Escaping Xavier

A DARK ROMANCE

LASHER BROTHERS DUET
BOOK TWO

MAE K. KNIGHT

Escaping Xavier

Xavier Lasher breaks out of prison with one goal: Claim his nurse, Lauren, as his.

Six years ago, I killed my father.

Four years ago, my twin nearly killed himself.

Now, I'm done waiting. I'm done serving time for a man the world doesn't miss.

And I'm done pretending that Lauren isn't mine.

I will have my freedom, and I will have my obsession. The only drug I'll ever need.

But when outside forces threaten to tear us apart, will she come back to me? And do I possess the courage to let my little Angel fly?

I don't know and I'm not eager to find out. So, I'll hold my Angel tight until I can feel her in my bones. Until her heart takes the shape of me.

If anyone tries to tear her from me, then the world better hope it's ready for another Lasher to stalk its streets. *I will not lose her.*

Contents

Also by Mae K. Knight iii

Escaping Xavier 1
Disclaimer 5
Author Note 6
Trigger Warnings 7
Playlist 9
The Murder 13
1. Escaping 17
2. Waking Up 20
3. The Devil 22
4. Humility 24
5. A Light Snack 26
6. All Dirty 28
7. Xavier's Game 31
8. Tempting the Devil 33
9. Obsession 35
10. Eat, Lauren 37
11. Don't Run 40
12. Breaking Mine 42
13. The Past Haunts 44
14. Happy Ending 47
15. The Claiming 50
16. Freedom 54
17. Escape 56
18. Rides and Reunions 58
19. Stalked 62
20. Stalker 66
21. Another Game 70
22. Claimed 73
23. Good Behavior 76

24. Family Ties   81
25. Breakfast for Four   85
26. Accomplices   87
27. Lasher Twins   90
28. Meeting The Family   92
29. She's Mine   95
30. Baby Incoming   99
31. Third Lasher   100
32. Hello, Zaria   102
33. Escaping Xavier   104
34. On Your Knees   106
35. Let Him Beg   108
36. King in Check   113
37. We're A Family   116
    Keeping Xavier   119
    Excerpt   120

    Acknowledgments   123
    About the Author   125

Disclaimer

Hi, lovely reader. I want to put a small disclaimer here (ahead of the trigger warnings on the next couple of pages).

As a reader, I understand the disappointment of picking up a book and it's not at all what you expected. I would not want any reader to be misled by my blurb.

If you read Surviving Zaine, which I recommend, and thought to yourself "this is more smut than plot," then this novella might not be for you.

I enjoy writing character focused stories with a plot as background noise. The spice in here might not be smut level, but if you're looking for a grand, complex plot, then you will be disappointed.

Spare both of us by putting this one back on the shelf until you're lookin' for something a little spicy that doesn't require a whole lot of thinking or following along.

Love,

Mae.

Author Note

This book contains explicit adult content. It is not for anyone under 18 years of age. This book is morally grey at best, a dark romance at worst and does contain sensitive material that may be triggering to some.

It is never my intent to do harm, so please take care of yourself and read the following warnings. They may contain spoilers, but if this book is not for you, please close and throw away. No book is worth your mental health.

Trigger Warnings

This book contains sensitive material relating to:
Anxiety
Addiction
Anal Play
Assault
Blood
Breath Play
Knife Play
Depression
Childbirth (Not FMC)
Incarceration
Murder
Parental Death
Kidnapping
Pregnancy
Dubious Consent
Nonconsent
Physical child abuse
Self-harm

Sexual abuse
Sexual assault (mentioned, not in detail)
Suicide
Somnophilia

Playlist

Mansion — NF, Fleurie
    Desire — Violet Orlandi
    Stalker — Stevie Howie
    Disturbia — Rihanna
    Straitjackets & Roses — Diggy Graves
    Seven Devils — Florence + The Machine
    Like You Mean It — Steven Rodriguez
    Tattoo — Loreen
    Who Do You Want — Ex Habit
    These Arms of Mine — Otis Redding
    Sweet Dreams (Are Made Of This) — Marilyn Manson
    I Put A Spell On You — Marilyn Manson
    Sweet Dreams — Beyonce

Dedication

For the dark girlies fantasizing about an unhinged murderer escaping from prison and kidnapping his obsession. This one is for you. Enjoy.

The Murder

PROLOGUE

XAVIER

I stare down at my father's lifeless body, blood spreading in a pool from his neck. My phone buzzes in my pocket. Pulling it out, blood staining my knuckles, I check the name calling. Xander.

Numbness spreads from my chest, clicking the green answer button.

My cousin's soft-spoken voice comes over the line. "Zay, what the hell's going on with you? I've called you like five times." My eyes bore into my father's prone form, images of fists and broken beer bottles coming at me, invading my mind.

Through a hoarse throat, I croak, "He's dead, Zan. I killed him. I finally fucking did it." My legs give out, forcing me to kneel beside the dead man who terrorized my family for years.

"Zay. You're not saying what I think you're saying, are you?" Xander's voice doesn't waver. He's steady like that, always a rock for me to lean on, bearing my fucked-up weight. I've lost count how many times the guy pulled me out of trouble over the years. And I've finally done the ultimate fuck-up.

My head pounds, consequences finally clicking in my mind. I'm not smart enough to get away with murder. My mind spirals, thoughts of who will look after my mentally unstable mother and straight as an arrow twin.

"Stay wherever the fuck you are, Zay. I'll do research on the way. I've got you. If anyone asks, it was self-defense. There's enough police calls over the years to back it up—"

"I slit his throat," I interrupt my cousin to say.

"Fuck," Xander breaths on the phone, but doesn't lash out at me, silence taking over his line. I keep kneeling in blood, letting him think. That's Xander, the smart one. He used some of the money from his father's life insurance to start up his own computer software company.

"Ok. Stay put, I'm still coming," Xander finally says, before adding, "And don't you fucking call Zaine or your mother. Let the police tell them. You and I will protect them the best way we can from this. I'm hacking the police system now, making the domestic violence reports public knowledge. I'll call one of my classmates in journalism to re-release the article about my dad's death in the drunk driver accident to drive up sympathy." Tension eases in my chest, my eyes finally taking in the room around me.

My father's blood stains the Persian rugs beneath us. His L shaped wooden desk glares at me accusingly. Numb fingers click the end call button, Xander's voice still echoing on the line, listing more plans.

Metal glints in the light coming from the chandelier in the ceiling. My feet carry me to the fireplace near the paneled office door. Calloused fingers wrap around it, hatred and anger surging within my chest. I march over to the desk that chipped away at this family, gnawing my father alive inside, his work obsession and alcoholism depriving us of the family life we should have had.

I don't think, my arms swinging the poker down, metal crashing into wood. Splinters fly in the air, a sick satisfaction filling me. I hate this room, this house, and I loathe the man bleeding on the floor. My arms keep swinging, wrecking the desk like my father wrecked our family, like the drunk driver wrecked him by killing his twin.

I don't remember screaming, until a voice shouts over my own, running feet registering in my ear. I turn to see Xander standing near my dad's body. For the second time that night, I crumple to the floor, sobs wracking my body.

Xander rushes at me, holding me like my mother used to, talking in soothing tones. We both freeze when sirens break through the quiet. Xander's tension mirrors my own, both of us looking around the room with a worried gaze.

"It's okay," Xander reassures me. "I'll get you out no matter how long it takes. Didn't I say I'll always look after you?" My eyes find his, noting that the color is a twin of my own. I nod numbly, trusting my cousin, who never lets me down, unlike the dead body lying several feet away from us.

"Get out of here," I croak, not wanting him caught with me. He can't help me if we're both in jail. He agrees, reluctance twisting his face, neatly combed dark hair shifting out of place when he runs a hand through it.

"Okay. Don't do anything stupid," he says, before looking at my dad. "Anything more stupid than that," he corrects himself, rising to his feet, dusting off his khakis.

I watch his lean form briskly walk out of the office, careful to not step in blood. Resting on my knees, I sit there in the silence of my childhood home, waiting for the police to arrive.

Escaping

XAVIER

ONE

I lie on the thin mattress on the bottom bunk, listening to the click of the guards' shoes patrolling, making sure everyone complied with lights out. Creaking above me lets me know my roommate is changing positions, getting comfortable. Wheezing from him brings a sick smile to my lips. He and a few of his friends tried cornering me in the yard. I got a week in solitary, daily visits from my favorite nurse; he got three cracked ribs and predatory gazes feasting on him for weaknesses. I give him a week before they find him bleeding out in the bathroom. He should've picked a weaker opponent.

Taking Dad's punches helped toughen me up. Half of the so-called tough guys in here are comfortable. They've spent too much time adjusting to routine, spoon fed instructions, using numbers to bully the weak. I grin down at my healing knuckles. I guess I learned how to throw a few punches of my own.

When I think of Nurse Lauren, my grin gets bigger. The time in the yard was well-spent, despite some of the licks I took. I know Lauren works late, leaving well past the time she should. I've bribed guards before to sneak out and see her. She denies there's anything between us, because I'm in here and she's out there. Well, that will soon change. She will be mine.

My hand makes its way into my jumper, resting over the right side of my heart. My twin, Zaine, has the same tattoos as me on his chest. Angel wings, the arches kissing our collarbone. One wing per brother. The one on the right is for Zaine. The other is for our little brother, Zaiden, who died from SIDS. Sudden Infant Death Syndrome took him from us. Triplets pulled apart by the cruelties of life.

Mom said dad used to be happy. He started drinking after Zaiden's death, then his twin died in a car accident. Zaine and I were never sure if she knew how often he rained punches down on us, me jumping in front of Zaine to take the brunt of it. Now, the fucker rests six feet under and I'm serving a lesser sentence for murder. But don't worry, little brother, I'm getting out of here. Six years is plenty of time spent being punished for someone the world doesn't miss. I'm sure Zaine took care of mom, helping her recover from her worsening addiction. If he didn't, well, I'm coming home.

Right on cue, all hell breaks loose. Show time, boys.

~

When the power shuts off with a quiet hum, doors sliding open, all hell breaks loose. The pounding steps of guards flood the cells. I don't make my escape amid the confusion. I strip off the orange jumpsuit, drop to my hands and knees, pulling an all-black pair of clothes from beneath my bunk. My cousin, Zachariah, who shut off the power, told me I'd have about fifteen minutes before the emergency generators come online.

Raised voices erupt from all around me. Even my roommate scurries out of his bunk, taking a chance at freedom. I scoff at him. They won't make it far without a badge. Good thing I know a certain nurse works late tonight. I won't go the usual route they'd expect an escapee to go. I'm not leaving without Lauren.

Shoeless, I pad softly out of my cell, weaving in between the crush of bodies. Guards single-mindedly focus on anyone wearing orange. I'm barely spared a glance in the near complete darkness, red flashing lights illuminating the area at infrequent intervals. Rough stone scrapes the bottom of my feet, and I eye one guard in the middle of a scuffle with a couple of inmates. Sneaking closer, lowering myself to the ground, my hand snatches out for his badge when one guy clocks him hard across the jaw.

Then I'm bouncing out of the way, hurrying toward Lauren's clinic.

Waking Up

LAUREN

TWO

I blink bleary eyes open, my heart freezing in my chest instantly. Tugging on my arms, I gasp, looking up at the iron chains looped around a wooden beam supporting the ceiling and wrapping around my wrists. A quick glance down reveals I'm still clothed in the black scrubs I wore to work before waking up wherever the hell I am. I'm fighting back a whimper, trying to pull up my last memory, but fear paralyzed my brain cells.

My toes barely scrape the wooden floor beneath my feet, blood pooling in my joints, and my wrists ache from the chains. Whatever hell I've woken up in, I want out. Pushed up into a corner is a lonely twin mattress that's seen better days, a ratty brown blanket sprawled on top. My head swivels to the left, noting the wooden window frame sporting a blacked-out window. It reveals nothing about my location. The room lacks decorations or functional furniture except for the bed, and a musty smell hangs in the air as if no one's lived here for years.

Tears sting my eyes. I'm fearful of crying out for help in the event it alerts my captors that I'm awake. I assume there's a door to my back since I can't see one anywhere else in the small room. The floor creaks beneath me, tensing my limbs.

My tormentor is with me.

The Devil

LAUREN

THREE

Panting, fear squeezing my lungs, I wait for my captor to reveal themselves. Almost languidly, footsteps edge closer, each creak sending a jolt of terror through me. I shriek when a hand lands on my hip, breath kissing my nape. I still don't know who's behind me.

"Good morning, doll. You've been sleeping awhile," a familiar voice rasps in my ear. Xavier? But—That can't be. He's an inmate, locked in a cell patrolled by armed guards. Hazy memories of alarms blaring, red lights flashing, and sprinting to my car assail my mind. I don't remember getting into the car. Everything went dark.

"Xavier," I breathe, realizing the cause of my lapse in memory, sluggish limbs, and dry mouth. He drugged me, probably used my keys to unlock my car, throwing me inside and making an escape. It's the only explanation. That or I've lost my mind.

I feel soft lips curl against my skin. He's smiling, shifting closer and the hardened cock brushing my hip sends more fear pummeling through my veins. Kidnapped and raped, I can see it now in tomorrow's headline, just another statistic. I berate myself not for the first time for taking a job at a prison straight out of nursing school. To be fair, during the four years I worked there, nothing like this ever happened.

Tears swell in my eyes, spilling over, cascading silently down my cheeks. I won't give him the satisfaction of hearing my cry. My tears would probably excite him more than my fear does. My body remains tense, expecting the worst.

"Are you hungry, doll?" he asks, running his fingers up and down my hip. If it's intended to be soothing, it's not working, I think to myself, refusing to answer the question until he tells me why the hell I'm hanging from shackles.

He clucks his tongue chidingly before landing a hard smack against my ass. I cry unexpectedly, body swinging forward on the chains. My tears come faster. I bite my lip, bowing my head, expecting more blows that don't come.

"I asked a question, pet. Will you starve because of your stubbornness?" he asks in a casual voice.

"Fuck you, Xavier," I yell back. I hope he kills me so I can haunt his ass. He laughs, walking around my body until he's standing in front of me. I withhold a gasp. His startling blue eyes always unarmed me back in the prison. Right now, he's looking ravenous, letting those eyes peruse my bound body. Pale blonde hair, shaved on the sides, falls forward on his forehead. He pushes it back with an annoyed huff.

"Starve, it is then. I'll be back when you learn some humility," he says, smirking and sauntering off.

"Wait!" I cry, but a door shuts behind me, leaving me hanging with my thoughts.

Humility

LAUREN

FOUR

I hang there, iron cutting into my flesh, curling and uncurling bloodless fingers, hoping to promote the proper blood-flow. I give up trying to get my feet flat on the floor. He truly has me chained in the most uncomfortable way. He's probably hoping it'll break me. I don't waste my time screaming for help. I've seen his chart. They imprisoned him for the murder of his father.

I fight more tears, angry at myself for being deceived by a pretty face, expecting someone like him to be kind or empathetic. Memories of our brief conversations when I forgot we were patient and nurse flicker through my mind. He'd been the only kind prisoner, eager to talk with me, making me feel human. Now, he's kidnapped me.

My mind takes me back to the night he must have escaped.

~

I stretch my arms above my head, releasing a grunt, wincing at the loud popping of my joints. Getting old was a bitch. I try settling back into my computer chair, my pad chafing between my legs, pulling another wince, and I rub my eyes, sleep beckoning me *to return home, leave the charts for tomorrow. Blue eyes flash behind my eyelids and I pop them open, shoving Xavier's pale gaze from my mind. Out of all the prisoners, he unsettles me the most.*

Maybe it's the hungry look he gets when he thinks I'm not watching, or how he always seeks me out. Sometimes, I wonder if he gets hurt on purpose, just to stop in the clinic, asking personal questions we both know I'm not allowed to answer. After every examination, he listens intently to my discharge instructions, gaze fixed on my lips. Then he'll give me a smirk before sauntering out the door, as if to say see you next time, doc.

Infuriating man, I think with a huff, turning back to my computer, vision blurring from staring into a digital screen for several hours. Just as I resume transcribing my notes into the patient's chart, alarms blare, red flashing lights searing my eyes, and my computer screen goes dark. What the hell? I rise from my seat, overhearing raised voices down the hall. Fear, slick and insidious, worms its way into my body.

Absently, I grab my white coat off the back of my chair, heart racing, wiping sweaty palms on my pants, and approach the door with weak legs. I've worked at this site for the last four years. During that time, a prisoner never escaped. The staff practiced drills, but my mind goes blank, fear paralyzing my brain cells.

Running feet pound down the hall. A frightened whimper slips from me. I force my legs to carry me to the door, cautiously opening a crack to assess the scene in the hall. Several guards march past my door in a hurry, barely sparing me a glance. They're headed toward the cells. Logic tells me the safest place is inside the prison. If someone is escaping, then being outside is the greatest risk. But panic urges me to run out the door, phone and keys in each hand, sprinting to the exit.

FIVE

I must have fallen asleep because the next time I open my eyes, I'm staring up at the ceiling. A shocked moan slips from me and I glance down wide eyed at Xavier. Both of my legs are resting on his shoulders, my pussy pressed into his face. He makes a greedy sound when he notices I'm awake, never stopping his feast, fingers tightening on my thighs. My hips roll involuntarily against his face, chasing his tongue, which flicks my clit eagerly. I'm too turned on to be embarrassed by the blood I see staining his shirt.

I was asleep. No one asked him to eat me out, blood and all. A wave of pleasure rolls into me and I'm crying out, coming on Xavier's tongue, whimpering when he sucks my clit between his lips, aftershocks wracking my body. When I finally quit twitching, he sits back on his heels, beaming a smile at me, blood coating his chin. I'm too shocked to do anything except stare.

He wipes a careless hand across his mouth, rubbing my blood on his thigh, hunger still burning in his eyes. I realize he could've done anything to me while I slept. All I can think is what now?

Xavier slides my open legs off his shoulders, one at a time, almost reluctantly.

"Are you ready to eat or still being stubborn? Because, I have to say, that was quite a snack for me." His words bring a flush to my face. No guy had ever gone down there while I was bleeding. Blood obviously doesn't bother Xavier.

Silently, I watch him grab my scrub bottoms off the floor, eyes flicking from them to me. Grinning evilly, he tosses them away from me, letting them land in an ungraceful heap a few feet away.

"Let's leave those off for now. You didn't answer my question again. Shall I repeat the lesson from earlier about what happens when you don't answer me?" I shake my head, not wanting his hands anywhere near my naked lower half now that the haze of lust cleared.

"Can I have my pants back? Or my panties, at least?" I ask, not meeting his eyes.

"No." He rises to his feet, my eyes landing on the thick imprint straining the denim jeans molding his muscular legs.

Hurriedly, I reply, "No, I'm not hungry," ignoring the tightness in my stomach. Xavier gives me a look of disbelief, snorting.

"Suit yourself. I'll give you some more time alone." His lips stretch wider. "Maybe I'll wake you up with something else next time." My heart sinks at those ominous words. I fight more tears, watching him stride away from me, aiming for the door at my back.

When I hear the door click close, my bravado crumbles, letting out tearful sobs. I don't know how much more of this I can take. There's no clock adorning the wall, depriving me of any concept of time. I'm afraid I'll break long before he does.

All Dirty

LAUREN

SIX

I cry myself to sleep, but jolt awake during odd intervals, adrenaline and fear constantly zinging through my veins. My arms quickly lose sensation, pins and needles traveling down to my shoulders. Upon waking again, I fight more tears, glancing down at the puddle of blood pooling beneath my feet. My thighs itch, caked with dried blood.

A noise from my right instantly has me tensing up, glancing over to find Xavier watching me from the thin twin mattress. He's naked, body splayed out, trailing a hand down, lazily stroking his cock. The shitty lighting in the room kisses every dip and groove of the muscled specimen, gazing at me with hooded eyes. I catch the names of Zaine and Zaiden on his chest before he's shifting into an upright position.

"Glad you're awake, doll. Looks like you'll be needing a bath. All that blood won't clean itself." He rises to his feet as he talks, my eyes losing a fight against the urge to stare. Full lips smirk at me, causing shame to flush my body. His hard cock bobs with every step toward me, drawing my eyes like a moth to a flame.

Looking at him and the weapon between his legs brings back memories of his slick tongue sliding through my folds. I shut my eyes against the memories, fighting my body's reaction. The floorboards creak beneath his soft steps, sending more tension through weak limbs. My whole-body aches, dried blood itching and irritating my skin, and my stomach growls with hunger.

Fatigued, I wait for Xavier's next move, feeling too weak to put up a fight. His breath comes out in a snorted huff, footsteps padding away from me. Wood complains as something scrapes across the floor, forcing my eyes to snap back open. Xavier is behind me, out of my line of sight. More tears spring to my eyes, just when I thought I was all cried out.

"Please," I whisper, throat clogged with unshed tears. The not knowing gnaws at me, like the growing hunger in my stomach. I don't know how much time has passed since he's taken me, or what he'll do to me when he's done with this sick game. Bile churns in my stomach, threatening to crawl up my throat, and fear tightens my chest.

Feeling something brush against me, I release a scream, and swing my body forward on my chains. Xavier chuckles, metal clanking behind me, my feet slowly lowering to the ground. Weak legs are unable to support me, trembling from lack of proper blood-flow. Xavier keeps lowering the chains until my arms are able to come down to rest at my side.

Cool wood presses against my cheek. I lay prone against the floor, letting my body adjust to being horizontal. Pale feet stride in my line of sight.

"You're all dirty, doll. Let's get you cleaned up." He kneels down, scooping me up into his arms with little effort. I lie limp against his chest, his heartbeat thumping in my ear, warm skin kissing mine. I'm too weak, too tired to do more than let him carry me through the bedroom door into a semi illuminated hall. Light shines from a cracked door on our right.

Xavier stalks in the light's direction, humming beneath his breath. The swaying motion of being carried combined with the fresh blood circulating through my body causes my eyes to droop. I don't realize I'm dozing off until I'm startled by running water.

Xavier sits on the lip of an off-white porcelain tub, one arm supporting my body while I rest in his lap, the other hand swirling through the water, testing the temperature.

I don't move, afraid to even breath with his cock resting beneath my bottom, skin to skin with my folds. A noise must escape me, Xavier's head swiveling back down in my direction, lips curled upward.

"Ready for a bath?" he asks huskily. My scrub top shields my upper body from view. A squeak slips past my lips when I realize Xavier's other hand rests against my mound. He pets my dark curls absently, one brow cocked at me.

"Can I bathe alone?" I ask, wishing I could disappear or have the strength to fight him off.

His lips draw my eye when they widen into a bigger grin. "I think you know the answer to that. Is this the part where you become stubborn again? Compliance looks good on you." I watch his pale eyes brighten with excitement. Instinctively, I know he wants me to put up a fight; he craves the high of being in control, dominating another.

I've seen his type. He fooled me in the prison with amiable smiles, light conversations, and a cocky demeanor. But, just like the other inmates, darkness lurks in his eyes, swimming through his veins. Whatever he hopes to get from kidnapping me, I swear to not give it to him, even if it kills me.

Xavier's Game

LAUREN

SEVEN

Biting my lip, I look away from Xavier, giving him a quick shake of my head. He leans over, shutting off the water, neck inches from my face, letting his musky scent waft over me. Sweat, blood, and something reminiscent of muscadine swirls together in an odd mixture. I glance down at my blood caked thighs, the outline of Xavier's cock peeking through the gap.

My eyes drift up toward his face, finding him already watching me. He blinks, schooling his features, but I saw the raw hunger carving his face. I fight a chill threading down my spine. Shifting in his lap, ignoring his choked groan from my nether lips sliding over his cock, I slip into the bathtub.

A glance over my shoulder reveals a slack-jawed Xavier. He hadn't expected me to slide off him, brushing my pussy against his cock in the process. My eyes shift from him to the toilet on the right, the empty towel rack attached to the cream walls and back to him.

"Do you have clothes?" I ask. "Or tampons," I mumble, watching the water stain red. Xavier clears his throat, standing, glancing at the specks of blood adorning his legs, courtesy of me.

"No tampons, but I—" He breaks off, like he'd almost admitted something. "I've got us some clothes," he finally says, which I suspect is a lie. My instincts tell me he has an accomplice. How else could he have gotten out of the prison and kidnapped me?

I pull my legs up to my chest, laying my cheek on my knees. My eyes drift shut as Xavier's footsteps pad away from the bathtub and out of the door. I contemplate making a run for it, but the state my body is in after hanging from my arms for hours, I wouldn't make it far. I'd only piss off Xavier, enduring whatever punishment he picks for me. Dampness coats my face, more tears sliding free, splattering onto my bent knees.

I'm too tired to tense when I hear Xavier returning, undoubtedly with stolen clothes. Clothes rustle and I peek at him, placing towels with tags still attached on top of the lid of the toilet seat. I bite my lip, burying my face into my knees when I see him turn around, intending to join me in the bathtub.

Ripples disturb the water, his legs brushing mine. I stay curled in on myself, listening to him getting settled into the too small bathtub, his legs bracketing mine on either side.

When my toes brush his cock, I jerk back, snapping my eyes up to his. A salacious grin graces his face.

"Don't tell me you've given up, doll. I thought you had more spirit," he taunts, arms braced on either side of the bathtub. I eye him critically, trying to think my way through the best solution to dealing with him. Clearly, he has no intention of letting me go. He's stronger than me so he could easily overpower me if I tried escaping.

My eyes dip to his cock bobbing in the water inches above my feet. Revulsion rolls through me, but so does determination. They say the best way to deal with the devil is to beat him at his own game.

Tempting the Devil

LAUREN

EIGHT

I can do this, I think, trying to hype myself up. Uncurling my legs, I place one on either side of his hips. Xavier's eyes widen slightly, lips parted on a gasp. Feeling emboldened, I scoot forward, ass sliding against porcelain, until I'm straddling Xavier.

I watch with fascination as his pupils dilate, chest rising and falling with rapid breaths. His cock jerks between us eagerly. He watches, waiting to see what I'll do next. I decide to go for gold, leaning down, brushing my lips softly across his in a featherlight kiss. He groans, hands snapping down to hold my hips, pressing me against his cock.

"What are you doing, angel?" he whispers, breath fanning my lips. I smile, his reaction fueling the feeling of addictive power. My hips rock back and forth, my nether lips sliding over his cock. A moan slips from both of us, panting against each other.

"You play a dangerous game," he murmurs, eyes drifting closed. I know, I want to say. But, I only have so many cards to play for my freedom. If I have to whore myself out to get out of here alive, I'll fuck the devil.

My teeth nip his lips, my hips picking up momentum, the tip of his cock hitting my clitoris on each slick glide. Xavier groans, tightening his hold, rocking his cock against me, sliding through my folds without entering me. He moves his head, lips trailing across my neck. Fuck, this shouldn't feel good, I think, chasing another orgasm with my kidnapper. His cock feels sublime, velvet poured over steel, the girth tantalizing me with images of being filled by him. I lean into the fantasy, whimpering with each stroke against my clit.

Fingers slide over my skin, trailing up toward my breast, flicking my beaded nipple. Xavier circles my hardened nipple, increasing the force of his thrusts against me, and I explode with a weak cry, just as his teeth sink into my neck, pain mingling with pleasure. His hands come back to their position on my hips, guiding me to keep grinding until my aftershocks fade.

The water cooled minutes ago, but we rest against each other, panting. I'm still in disbelief that I did that.

Obsession

LAUREN

NINE

Xavier brings up a hand, tangling his fingers in my hair with an apt expression on his face. My lips curl against his chest. It's as if he's never played with a woman's hair before, particularly curly hair. It weaves around his fingers with each twirl. He tugs on it lightly, a soft smile curling his lips.

I rebel against the warmth spreading in my chest at the simplistic pleasure of Xavier toying with my hair. The childish joy in such a minor act threatened to thaw the barrier guarding my heart. I have to remind myself that he kidnapped me, shoulders still tender from hanging from a damn ceiling. I refuse to succumb to Stockholm Syndrome, softening toward my kidnapper.

"Are you ready to eat now?" he asks in a soft voice, still raptly playing with my hair. A question ping-pongs through my mind, refusing to rest.

"Why did you kidnap me?" I ask, fearful and hopeful of the answer. His chest rises, stalls, then lets out the breath he held. The shower reverberates from his head thudding against the wall, resignation twisting his lips. His finger remains curled in my hair.

"I need you, pet," he confesses to open air, eyes closed. My brows shift downward quizzically.

"What—"

"I need you like I need air to breathe. You were literally the rising sun and setting moon for me since the first time our paths crossed. I broke out, but couldn't leave my heart behind. So," he sighs, a pained expression flitting across his face. "So, we're hiding out here until the police lessen the intensity of their search. I wish I could say I'd let you go, but I'm a selfish bastard, like my dad. Death will come for me long before I allow myself to let you go." His confession weighs down the air I breathe, constricting my lungs. I can't believe the depth of his obsession.

Silence settles among us, an uncomfortable, stifling blanket. Deciding I'd had enough, I reach behind Xavier, releasing the lever to allow the water to drain. He doesn't comment, sitting still beneath me. Resolute to test the waters further, I slowly rise to my feet, a blush coloring my cheeks when I glance down at Xavier's head below my naked thighs.

I step out of the bathtub, snatching up a towel. My flimsy shield soaks up the water from my body. My ears pick up Xavier rising behind me, water splashing down into the bathtub from his movements. Keeping my back to him, towel wrapped around my body, I wait for his next move.

My lips twitch at the wry thought of us playing a game of chess. I suspect he'd have my king in check in no time.

Eat, Lauren

LAUREN

TEN

Water patters to the floor in gentle droplets, soft pellets caressing my overstimulated senses. Xavier's body heat warms my back when he approaches, closing the distance between our bodies. Damp skin slides against me, his hands gripping my hips, lips brushing over my ear.

"What will Lauren do next, I wonder? Hmm? Are you going to do more than just grind on my dick?" I jerk away from him, bravado failing, hands clutching my towel like a shield.

Xavier laughs, reaching down for his own towel leisurely, daring me to look away from his nudity.

"Who're Zaine and Zaiden?" Genuine curiosity spurs me to ask. Pale brows lift to his hairline.

"You actually want to get to know me, Nurse Lauren? Or are you just stalling?" Beneath the sarcastic taunt, notes of vulnerability slip through. My eyes narrow on him, mind flickering through various scenarios. I ponder if trying to reach the humanity buried within him would heighten his obsession, or provide me with an opportunity for escape.

I always hated chess. Shrugging my shoulders, I feign indifference. Xavier stands still, towel hanging low on his waist, distrust and indecision warring in his eyes.

"My brothers," he whispers before his eyes harden into shards of ice. "And that's all I'm saying on the subject. Now, let's eat. If you think you're going to get away from me so easily by starving to death, then, doll, I'd hate to disappoint you. But I'm not letting you die that easily, as amusing as it is watching you let your pride destroy you." He stalks forward and I side step to the right, gesturing with my hand toward the door.

"After you," I say demurely. Snorting a laugh, Xavier leads the way out of the bathroom. Dirty floorboards creak beneath our feet. I have the brief fear the floor will give out right as we're walking. The hallway isn't long, opening up into a sparsely decorated living room.

My nose crinkles at the furniture gracing the dusty floors. Cushions sag with their guts hanging out. Scarred wooden end tables act as bodyguards on either side of the lifeless sofa. Moonlight filters through dirty cracked windows. Xavier strides to a counter with greasy bags of fast food congealing on top.

My stomach rumbles and roils at the same time. I don't think I'll be able to keep down whatever poisoned food he purchased from Mickey D's. A frown turns his lips when he notices my reaction.

"Too good for fast food?" A veiled threat lurks in his voice.

"You don't have soup?" I ask, preferring anything over the grease sponge in that bag.

A muscle ticks in his jaw, nostrils flaring slightly. "If I had soup, Lauren, I would have heated it up. I don't know if you noticed, but this isn't the Ritz."

"No, it's a hellhole," I snap, my patience wearing thin. My eyes alight on the weathered door standing between me and freedom.

"Don't even think about it." Xavier prowls my way and I instinctively back up, a grimy wall meeting my back. I'm surprised used needles don't litter the floor of the abandoned heap he kept me locked up in.

Xavier closes the distance between us, long legs moving swiftly across the room. He pauses in front of me, glaring down into my eyes. Lifting my chin, I glare back, silently daring him to hit me. He doesn't, but his lips twitch with a smile. I guessed right about his desire for dominance. Just like animals in nature culling the weak, nurses eat their young, and if we weren't in the middle of nowhere with no one knowing my whereabouts, I'd be a lot less fearful of him.

"Do you want to say something, doll? Cat got that sharp tongue of yours?" he whispers, leaning closer, skin brushing mine. Inhaling sharply, I shrink back against the wall. Xavier's eyes track the movement, anger sparking before fizzling out. He wants a fight, not a cowering mouse. I wonder if that's what drew him to me. Working in a prison filled with hardened criminals meant I had to grow tough skin and give as good as I got. Movement below the waist draws my eye to his cock, hardening again behind his towel.

Jerking my eyes back up reveals a derisive grin stretching Xavier's face. Lights flash through the window, eliciting a gasp from me. Breath leaves me when Xavier slams his body into mine, hand coming up to cover my mouth, cock pressing into my stomach.

"Don't you fucking breath a word," he snarls, fury etching the angular lines of his face.

Don't Run

LAUREN

ELEVEN

Frozen in terror, I blink unshed tears, fearful of breaking eye contact with Xavier, a tense barricade pressed against me. Tires crunch over gravel, headlights illuminating the interior of the dilapidated shack. Rapid breaths burst from Xavier, pale eyes shifting from me to the door, tensed limbs tightening against me.

A car door opens, loud as a gunshot in a quiet woodland. A whimper gets trapped against Xavier's hand, and he leans closer, eliminating any space between our bodies.

"Don't test me, pet. I'd hate to do it, but I would snap that pretty neck before I allow someone else to have you. Don't make a fucking sound." My head nods weakly against his hand, my tears streaking down to stain his skin. I'm paralyzed by shock when he eliminates the space between our faces, sticking his tongue out to lick my tears.

My pussy pulses when he whispers, "Delicious," breath fanning my wet cheeks. Both of our heads swivel to the door when shoes crunch on gravel.

A masculine voice rings out. "Zay! Get your ass out here." I sob against his hand, piss oozing out of me, dribbling down my leg.

Xavier returns his attention to me, glancing down at the mess I'm making.

His eyes widen, relaxing his hold. "Damn, pet. My cousin terrifies you more than me?" he asks, brows dropping low over his eyes.

That's it. My nervous system short circuits and I sag against Xavier, crying loud enough to wake the dead. Adrenaline leaves me weak, trembling in Xavier's arms. He hugs me tightly, kissing my forehead and hair, murmuring "I've got you", over and over.

Breaking Mine

LAUREN

TWELVE

A ceiling caked with dust, cobwebs, and water stains glares down at me. I lie in Xavier's arms, letting a numbness seep in. The door to freedom creaks open, but I remain mesmerized by the ceiling, unable to look away. Xavier whispers something above my head, the words slithering into one ear and out the other.

Another voice answers him, my eyes wondering to the newcomer. He has Xavier's eyes, I think to myself, smiling ridiculously. The stranger's lips turn down, piercing eyes roaming over me. I almost forget the piss souring the air, coating my legs, and staining Xavier's feet. My captor doesn't appear to mind, replying to his cousin in a rapid fire of words. An argument ensues and I return my gaze to the ceiling, watching one particular stain spread.

I jolt when lips trail across my forehead, traveling down my nose and brushing my lips. I melt into Xavier's kiss, letting his tongue tangle with mine, moaning at the slightly minty taste that I overlooked earlier. My hands reach up, winding through his blonde hair, pulling him down to me and deepening the kiss.

I cannot think, and it feels amazing. His mouth ravages mine, preventing my senses from returning. My nipples rub against the fabric of the towel, wetness pooling between my thighs.

Xavier pulls his mouth from me, causing a pout to twist my lips. I want more.

"No, angel. You're not yourself. Trust me, I want you screaming my name. But—" He shakes his head, hair sweeping across his forehead. "I don't want it like this. You need some rest, proper rest. I didn't think my cousin would be the one to break you, but—" His voice cracks before carrying on. "Come back to me, doll. I need that fire of yours to warm us both." Soft lips press against my forehead, tears sting my eyes. I don't know why, but the words worm into my chest, wrapping around my heart, squeezing the life out of me.

His words demand something from me. I shut my eyes, trying to block out the panic swimming in my veins.

"Lauren," I hear his voice enunciate, caressing the vowels in my name. They slide over his tongue so easily, I think to myself, wishing my name sounded horrible coming from his lips. Sensations return to my limbs, itchy cloth wrapped around my body, thighs irritated from urine.

"I need another bath," I croak. My throat tries tamping down emotions, feelings scraped raw. Xavier nods, rising to his feet, cradling me in his arms. I listen to his feet sliding across creaking wood, lulled by the sway of being carried. Darkness reaches for me before he makes it to the bathroom.

The Past Haunts

XAVIER

THIRTEEN

Wood creaks beneath my feet. I pace from one end of the small, barren bedroom to the other. Lauren rests on the thin mattress, dark hair haloing her angelic face. I'm glad dirt doesn't touch her, tampering with the pristine image.

I really fucked up, is all I can think. I nearly choked the life from the one male that ever cared to look after me. Xander's red, flushed face flickers in my mind, soft skin giving beneath my calloused hands. Betrayal sparks in eyes the same shade as mine, nostrils flaring. He doesn't fight me, lying underneath my weight like he's sunbathing or some shit. I shove the image away, but the voices won't relent.

"Get over here, you little shit!" a voice slurs in my head, tripping over the words. My hand curls into fists. Fortunately, they're not bloody and haven't been since capturing my angel. She's supposed to be my salvation, but I'm not so sure anymore. Seeing her unconscious body, mind in shambles, I snapped, tackling Xander to the ground.

"Stupid," I whisper under my breath, feet imitating my thoughts, walking in circles.

"You'll never amount to anything," that voice whispers, pricking my skin to seep beneath the layers. I bring the heels of my palms to press into dry eyes. I pull images of Lauren's soft smile and kind brown eyes to combat my father's poison. Wishing I'd discovered her during the worst of it, I soak up the warmth the memories of her provide.

Lauren's my obsession, but I'm supposed to care for her. Less than a week and I've already broken my doll. Guilt gnaws on my insides, taunting me with my father's cold blue eyes. He smiles viciously in my mind, blood painting his face and knuckles as I lay in a crumpled heap at his feet.

I remember being grateful, witnessing Zaine's sleeping form huddled in the bottom bunk of the twin bed we share before tip-toeing downstairs to greet the beast posing as my father. *He's worth it*, I used to remind myself, nose dripping blood, shooting my tormenter a bloody smile. I knew it'd enrage the bastard further, but did it anyway. If I tire the fucker out, he won't go after mom or Zaine.

My fist connects with the wall, past and present colliding. Chinks of drywall fall to my feet. I ignore the blood staining my knuckles. The brief bout of pain cannot satisfy the darkness settling around my heart. It whispers I'm better off drowning my angel in a pool of her own blood. I ignore the raspy, cruel voice. Lauren is mine and I will not allow any harm to so much as breathe on her dark curls.

Mine! I scream at the voices trying to swallow me whole. Lauren Bell is mine and I won't let my past torment me into hurting her. I'll break her in other ways, but none of her soft, brown skin will bare marks from my hands. Pleasure will burn her veins, clog her throat, but she'll never scream in pain, I vow to myself.

My feet carry me to the thin mattress cushioning my doll. I barely resisted not playing with her while I washed the piss from between thick, toffee thighs, her soft body resting in my arms. I loved the way her thighs molded around my hands, trying to trap me in the place as close to paradise a sinner like me can get.

I trail a finger down her cheek, watching the twitch of her eyebrows in fascination. Everything about her lures my eyes. I've never met someone as alluring as my angel. My hands twitch on her skin. Something dark and insidious whispers I'll taint her with my darkness. I ignore it, shoving it into a box. If I taint her, then I'll swallow her darkness whole, carrying it for the both of us.

Leaning down, I brush my lips across hers in a featherlight caress. She snorts a huff through her nostrils. Air kisses my skin and I inhale the breath she exhaled. My tongue begs to dip between her lips and feast on her again.

Later, I reprimand myself. I run a bloody knuckle across her mocha skin, letting the red stain her. I've broken my doll and don't deserve the pleasure of tasting her nectar on my tongue. If she awakes, feeling like herself, then I'll reward us both.

I slide across her, settling at her back before pulling her naked body into mine. She groans and her face twists, but she doesn't awaken. My cock nestles between her plump cheeks. My chin rests on the curve of her neck. Bliss blooms in my chest and I lean into the feeling, letting Lauren's allure beat back my father's voice.

My angel is the last thought ping-ponging in my head when sleep claims me.

Happy Ending

LAUREN

FOURTEEN

Moaning, I shift my hips against the fingers rubbing circles over my clit. Pleasure zings through me. I moan into the limp pillow beneath my head, musk filling my nose. Frowning, my eyes drift open, locking on the chains dangling from the wooden beam Xavier hung me from.

Gasping, pleasure crests over me, rolling my eyes back, coming against my captor's skilled fingers. Like fiddling with a flute, he presses the buttons to turn my body against me, even in my sleep. Lips caress my ear.

"Good morning, angel. How are you feeling? Better, I hope?" Huskiness taints his voice, sleep clogging his throat, deepening the rasp. A shiver travels down my spine from the sound.

I don't answer him, needing a moment to gather my thoughts and calm my overexcited hormones. Silky skin shifts against my butt cheeks, leaving a wet trail. I gasp, involuntarily pushing against the cock sliding over me. Xavier groans, gliding a hand down to ease his cock between my thighs. My pussy clenches at the sensation of his cock slipping through my lips, the mushroom tip teasing my clit. I'm melting against the bare chest at my back, rocking on the cock sliding along my pussy. Temptation urges me to shift my hips to impale myself on the thick length.

I barely resist, failing to suppress moans. His cockhead rubs me on each glide, the tip kissing my entrance, temptation riding him just as hard. I'm helpless against the onslaught, not complaining when the first inch breaches my walls only to retreat again, my juices staining the tip.

My nails dig into the arm wrapped around my chest, his fingers grazing my nipples. But Xavier focuses on edging us both, entering an inch, retreating, and repeating the action over and over. Soon, I'm tightening on air, his cock just out of reach on a retreat, liquid gushing between my thighs. His groan fills my ear, come splattering my thighs. I lay there in his arms, shocked and ashamed.

I'm losing count of how many times my kidnapper has made me come.

~

Xavier's breathing fills my ears, along with the rustle of cotton as he shifts closer, letting the tip of his cock rest against my opening.

"Hmm, how was that angel? You didn't answer my earlier question. Do you need another lesson on what happens when you don't answer me?" His lips tease my skin. One hand splayed across one butt cheek, fingers lightly tapping a warning.

I shake my head against the pillow, jostling his face.

"No," I whisper through a scratchy throat. Pale eyes and dark hair flash in my mind's eye.

"Your cousin helped you escape, didn't he?" Xavier's body stiffens, fingers pausing their idle drumming.

"Why do you want to know?" Fingers grip my face, turning me around to look into glacier eyes.

"What do you think of my cousin? Think he's some hero to

rescue you from me?" Demanding lips crush mine, claiming me in a bruising kiss, teeth nipping my lips.

"You're mine. My angel, my doll. Don't try to turn me against my cousin." Confusion stirs from his words. I pull tender lips away from his mouth.

"That wasn't what I was trying to do," I protest weakly, his lips returning to torment mine. Xavier hums, his hips shifting, dragging his cock along my lips again. Moaning into the kiss, ignoring the cum coating my thighs, I rock into him. My body ushers me to forget why this is wrong.

Warning bells ring in my head and I roll away, resting on my knees on the wooden floor. Xavier scowls, shifting to an upright position. Briefly, I consider running, eyes tracking the distance from the bedroom door to Xavier's kneeling position, mirroring my own.

Excitement flares in his eyes, lips curling.

"Go ahead," he encourages. "Run, see what happens when I catch you. And make no mistake, I will catch you, doll. My cousin isn't around, so don't expect any help from him." His mouth twists at the mention of his cousin. I sense jealousy and distrust churning through his sick mind.

I don't want to be punished. The distinct memory of pissing myself invades my mind. I rest on my heels, ass meeting the back of my calves. Xavier never dressed me, but he must have bathed me again.

My heart beats an unsteady rhythm, the thought of Xavier's hands sliding over my naked, vulnerable body, disrupting the pattern.

The Claiming

LAUREN

FIFTEEN

Calming my racing heart is a difficult feat. Xavier remains still, body tense and poised to give chase. Maybe I'm feeling a little reckless myself, because I'm rising to my feet, staring him down, letting my hatred burn in my gaze. He's right. I am feeling better, and I refuse to succumb to some Stockholm Syndrome bullshit.

Stagnant air caresses my hardened nipples, reminding me of what I let him do to me, of what my body still wants him to do. This is how it starts; I think. Returning a kiss, riding his cock, it all leads to being his, giving up on my hopes and dreams, everything I worked for.

Lauren Bell is no man's plaything. With that thought, I sprint for the door, pounding steps following close behind. Once I reach the door, I slam it behind me, straining my legs to put as much distance between me and Xavier.

An enraged yell follows me, sending chills down my spine, but I cross into the living room. Impulsively grabbing cushions, throwing them on the floor, toppling an end table. Then I sprint for the front door, a loud thud echoing behind me. I laugh when cool, fresh air kisses my face. I hope the fucker tripped.

The moon shines bright, illuminating the middle of nowhere,

secluded location a typical kidnapper would bring someone. Tire tracks litter the gravel, signs of Xavier's cousin. I hear Xavier behind me, heavy breathing and rapid steps.

I sprint across the yard, gravel abrading my feet, breasts bouncing with each step. It only occurs to me a few steps toward the woods that there might be worse monsters than Xavier. Reaching a wooded tree line, I risk a glance back. Xavier is hot on my trail, blonde hair flopping against his skull, cock bouncing against his stomach with each step.

I don't stop weaving in between trees, tears leaking freely. My feet complain with each step, rocks and sticks digging into my bare soles. Xavier doesn't bother with subtlety, crashing behind me, crunching through underbrush. My eyes dart around for a place to hide, or civilization, but come up empty. Trees surround me on all sides, limbs reaching for the sliver of moonlight breaking through the canopy.

"Lauren!" Xavier yells a few steps behind me, but coming from my left. I try watching my step, hoping stealth could be on my side. Maybe I could go around him, circle back to—

A hard body crashes into me, ripping a scream from my throat. I thrash and struggle against my captor, his naked skin sliding against mine, hardened cock leaving a damp trail. I yell in frustration, cursing him with every word I can think of. He laughs through it all, wrestling me on the forest ground, trying to subdue my flailing limbs.

He pins me beneath him, chest heaving from exertion. Sweat coats both of our skin, slicking the slide of his body against mine. Warm breath fans my ear when he leans down to taunt me.

"Told you I'd catch you, doll. Now, it's time to pay the piper. I'm claiming this pussy as mine." His words send frantic energy into me, renewing my struggles, his cock sliding along my butt cheeks. His laughter vibrates into my skin, the fight exciting him further. I sob into the leaves sticking to my face. I don't want this.

"Accept it, doll. This pussy is mine. You are mine."

"Fuck you," I scream into the dirt beneath my face. He leans closer, breath fanning my neck.

"No, doll, I am about to fuck you," he rasps against my skin.

Xavier spreads my thighs with his, thick fingers sliding through my lips when I'm exposed to him, eliciting a weak moan from me. He does it again, using my own wetness to circle my clit. My hips are rising off the floor, chasing his fingers. Xavier pinches my clit and I come in my captor's hand again, crying against the ground, whimpering from aftershocks when he returns to circle his fingers on me again.

I almost complain when he shifts his weight and removes his fingers, until something thick slides through my lips, soaking up my juices. My hips chase his cock greedily.

"You're such a good girl for me, doll, coming like that. Let me make us both feel good," he whispers, voice caressing my senses. I'm back to grinding my pussy lips against his cock, wanting the head to hit my clitoris like before. I moan into the ground, eyes twitching when the first thick inch glides inside me. My fingers reach for his, entwining our fingers, while he slowly fills me.

It's such a slick, easy slide, but he draws it out. My lips find his arm, teeth digging into him, hips rising to take more of him.

"Patience, doll," he groans in my ear. Fuck patience, I think. I shift my ass back more. He slips in another inch, yelling, "Fuck," before pushing forward and giving me all of him. Panting into the earth, his chest pressed into mine, we catch our breath, resting with him inside me. He lets me adjust to his thickness, but I'm feeling feral. If I'm going to fuck my kidnapper, then I want it hard and rough. This isn't lovemaking.

I clench around him, causing a hiss to escape him. Then I wiggle my ass, grinding on the cock inside me.

"Fuck, Lauren, be still." This time it's my turn to laugh.

"Don't think you're going to last long, champ?" I taunt him. Right before he growls, I briefly think, "maybe I shouldn't tease the devil."

His fingers untwine from mine, wrapping a hand around my throat. My eyes water, a choked moan coming out. His other hand finds my hip, pulling me up so my ass is in the air, his cock still inside me. Then he pulls his cock from me to the tip, surging back in. The hand on my throat restricts my airway, but I'm a moaning mess beneath him. Taking the pounding he starts; euphoria burns me when each thick inch edges closer to my cervix. This man is getting beneath my skin, burrowing into my body, and I'm helpless to stop it.

I'm writhing beneath him, dirt abrading my skin, teasing my nipples with the rough texture. Xavier eases his weight off me and I whimper at the loss.

"I'm not going anywhere, angel. This pussy is mine." A hard thrust punctuates his words. A hand comes down, slapping my ass and causing me to tighten around him. Xavier laughs evilly, soothing the hurt in the next second, massaging the skin, hips slamming into me with each thrust. My throat strains with a weak cry as pleasure slams into me, coming around Xavier's cock again.

His hand leaves my throat, both of them landing on either side of my head. No longer supporting my weight, Xavier uses his hands to support himself, increasing the pace of his thrusts. My eyes are rolling, walls clenching around him again with a weak climax. Xavier's grunts and the sound of flesh slapping breaks up the quiet of the surrounding trees.

His lips brush my ear as he whispers, "I'm coming, angel. Fuck, take all of me." He groans, cock pulsing inside me, pulling another orgasm from me. Xavier rests against me, and I close my eyes, laying limply beneath him, too weak to move.

I think that might have been the best sex of my life.

Freedom

LAUREN

SIXTEEN

I'm such a limp noodle, my cheek resting on the ground, eyes blinking sluggishly. I haven't eaten in God knows how long and just lost precious fluids. Xavier's cock definitely made me squirt, wetness coating my thighs, dribbling down my legs.

Xavier groans, dragging his cock out of me. I moan at the loss, tempted to wiggle and impale myself back on his thick member. Maybe he senses my thoughts because he laughs. He does that a lot, I realize. Now that I've had him in my body, I want to understand him and the shield he keeps up between him and everyone else, including me. Notes of vulnerability slipped through in our interactions, but I don't know him.

Tears fall freely as Xavier gently pulls me into his arms, walking us back to the shack. He looks down at my face, pausing.

"Shit, doll. You're all banged up. Was I too rough?" He genuinely appears concerned about that. I'm sure bruises decorate my neck and torso from being choked and fucked into the ground, but that's not why I'm crying. I shake my head, unable to will the tears away. He frowns, disbelief painting his face. I smile through my tears, wondering if my face looks as bad as I think it does.

"Angel—"

A shrill siren interrupts his voice. Xavier's head snaps toward the sound, arms tightening around me. He looks down at me, frowning, fear darkening his eyes.

"Xavier," I whisper, an unnamed emotion twisting my heart. His eyes roam over me, as if he's memorizing my face. He lifts me higher, claiming my lips possessively, wordlessly saying "mine" with each stroke of his tongue. I'm kissing him hungrily, weaving fingers into his hair, reluctant to let him go, but knowing what those sirens mean. Someone found us.

Xavier lowers me down to the ground, blue eyes looking brighter in the moonlight. I wonder if tears are brightening their hue.

"I've got to go, angel. I can't let them catch me." He kisses me again, lips pulling away slowly. "I'll find you," he promises. Tears sting my eyes as I watch him rise back to his full height, towering over me. My juices and his cum stain his cock. After having had it, I'm not sure I want to never be able to have him fill me again.

I blink rapidly, watching him run through the woods, pale taut ass cheeks reflecting the moon's glow. Hope is an ugly emotion in my chest. It splinters in two, one half hoping they catch him and the other half fearing the worst if they do.

I force my weak limbs to carry me back in the cabin's direction, toward the sirens. Trusting Xavier knows his way to the main road, I keep putting one foot in front of the other, ignoring the tears that keep falling the closer I get to freedom.

This is what I wanted, isn't it? That thought taunts me the entire walk back, standing naked, listening to the sirens increase in volume, signaling their closeness.

Escape

XAVIER

SEVENTEEN

Racing through the woods, butt ass naked and barefoot, is not my idea of fun, and I enjoy a few extremes, as my little angel will soon discover. I push my body to its fullest potential, running to put distance between myself and the shit storm I know will land at the shack where I held Lauren. Remembering her submission and cries of pleasure as she clenched around my cock, nearly causes me to stumble.

Xander told me something like this would happen, that I should've left her well enough alone. But my cousin had never been to jail a day in his life, toeing the straight and narrow, unless he's bailing me out of trouble. Then he develops some loose morals, like hacking into police filing systems or shutting down the power at a secured prison, stashing clothes, a map, a burner phone and a small amount of money just a couple miles outside of said prison.

If Xander had been in my shoes for even a moment, then he'd understand the draw to Lauren and her peaceful smiles, quick wit, sharp tongue, and expressive brown eyes. I didn't lie to her when I told her she became my entire world, the only bright spot in the hell-hole I survived in for six years. Six years of trying to keep my head down, staying vigilant for attacks, and praying for an early release for good behavior. Six years that got me nowhere. I needed Lauren's smile like an addict needed their next fix, willing to do anything to wind up in her clinic, experiencing her soft touch, hoping for more. Unrequited love is a bitch that I'd never recommend fucking.

Renewed appreciation for the computer genius filled me as I came up on a familiar tree, X carved into the base. Dropping to my knees, I dig into the loose dirt for the pack filled with another burner phone, sweats, a shirt, and after a quick count, I find one hundred dollars folded neatly in the sweatpants' pocket. My genius cousin only neglected shoes. I sigh, sitting on my heels, looking up at the stars. I would pray, but if the big guy cared, he'd have taken care of my father long before he started punching on his own sons. My hands clench, images of my mother's unconscious body laid on a bed, a stranger thrusting between her legs while my father watched.

I lean forward, stomach twisting at the images. Her addiction worsened throughout the years, but it never occurred to me or Zaine that our father would take advantage of her vulnerable state. I assumed he limited his abuse to his sons. How fucking naïve we were, I think with a sardonic twist of my lips, feeling his blood stain my skin all over again. Maybe that's why the psychiatrist never put in a word for early release, sensing my lack of remorse.

Shaking my head, feeling strands of hair brush my forehead, I rise to my feet with my prize, dressing quickly. I needed to find a new place to lie low, but most importantly, I needed to contact Xander and Zaine. Xander insisted we let the media and police inform my mother and brother about the jailbreak. But now that I'm free and having temporarily lost my doll, I might need Zaine's help. I stride around the tree, heading for the main road with renewed purpose. I hope my angel is getting ready for me because next time I'm not letting anything pry her from my greedy hands.

After all, I'm a selfish bastard, the son just like the father.

Rides and Reunions

XAVIER

EIGHTEEN

Silence chokes the air in the car, trees blurring by in the window. My shoulder blades rest against the sides of the passenger car door. I catch fleeting glances of traffic lights and a sky peppered with stars through the windshield, but I keep my face out of sight.

Leather creaks beneath Xander, dark hair standing up in spikes, silk pajamas catching the light at odd intervals. A sigh slips from me and Xander grunts from the driver's seat.

"The silent treatment is childish," I grumble, closing my eyes against the lights stabbing into them. How quickly I became used to being a creature of shadows.

"I hope she's worth it," Xander grits out, not looking in my direction. If the red handprints around his neck didn't make me feel like shit, I'd sock him for implying Lauren is anything less than perfection. She's worth any price life demands from me.

"Does Zaine know I'm coming?"

Silence answers me and my fingers curl into fists, blunt nails digging into my skin. I jerk my head back against the door, the dull ache of bone striking fiber glass softening the anger sparking inside of me.

Of course, Zaine doesn't know I'm coming. This night just keeps getting better and better. I sigh again, reliving claiming Lauren behind closed eyelids, hearing her moans caress my senses, pussy clenching around my cock. She's worth it. I can't wait to have my angel beneath me again.

~

My body jostles forward when Xander places the car in park. My head lifts with interest, curious eyes roving over the manse my twin calls home. Pale marble columns catch my eye, double French doors resting between the sentinels.

My heart ping pongs in my chest, sweat dampening my palms.

"Are you okay, Zay?" Xander asks softly. I shake my head, blinking tears away.

"He won't want to see me." The words trip from my lips. Lances of pain spear into my heart.

"I'll always protect you, Zaine. You hear me? Me and you. Remember that. Me and you." A phantom echo of my voice fills my ears. But I didn't protect him, did I?

My hands lash out, fist colliding with the dashboard.

"Fuck!" I scream at no one, throwing the door open, needing air. My lungs constrict with hunger.

A door opens and slams shut.

"Zay! Listen to me—"

"Why did you bring me here, Xander? He won't want to see me and I don't think I can see that after the fucking night I've had. I lost Lauren. I can't take anymore losses tonight." My voice cracks, throat clogging with emotions I try to tamp down.

The heels of my palms press into my eyes. I despise this feeling; the ground falling away from me, my father's voice creeping into my ears.

"What the fuck is going on here?" a familiar voice barks, jerking my head toward a face nearly identical to my own. Pale blue eyes widen, lips falling open in shock.

"Xavier?" Bare chested, moon light glides over the matching tattoo on his pecs. His chest moves up and down rapidly as he rakes his gaze over me.

"What the fuck are you doing here?" he asks after several tense moments of silence.

"He needs somewhere to lie low," Xander intervenes, stepping forward until he's nearly in the middle of both brothers.

"And you thought bringing him here was a good idea? He's my damn twin. This is the first place they'd look!" Spit flies from Zaine's lips. My feet carry me forward. I can lose my shit and attack Xander, but I draw the line at anyone else laying hands on the computer wiz.

"It was my idea," I lie. My eyes clash with Xanders and I jerk my head toward the car. He takes the hint, stepping back from Zaine.

Zaine's eyes snap to mine. Anger and betrayal swirl before shutters clamp down, shielding his emotions from me. I watch with nausea churning in my stomach as his face smooths out, leaving an implacable mask in place.

"You're putting my future wife and unborn child at risk. Keep to the guest room, stay away from the windows and—" he stalks closer, a fanatical look entering his eyes. "Stay the fuck away from Zoe or I'll slit your throat like you slit our fathers. And just like you, I won't have a shred of remorse for it."

Chinks of myself clatter to the metaphysical space of my heart. Numbness spreads from my chest and I give Zaine a weak nod, witnessing my fear come to life. A chasm stretches between us, two opposing forces and neither taking a step toward the other. Zaine jerks his head toward the house, door standing wide open before turning on a heel and stalking away.

"Zay," Xander whispers, the night air ferrying his words to me.

"Go home, Xander. You've done enough." Like Zaine, I don't spare him another look, feet carrying me after my twin.

I truly lost him, and Lauren. I can't risk looking back at Xander or I'd crumble like I did in my father's office. My cousins picked up my broken pieces often enough to last several lifetimes.

Tonight, I have to stitch myself together on my own.

Stalked

X & L

NINETEEN

XAVIER

Moonlight caresses skin reminiscent of rich cocoa. I can vouch for her tasting just as sweet. I trace circles in the air above Lauren's face. One touch and plans disappear up into smoke. Soft snorts seep through the door of her bedroom and I scowl in that direction.

Her mother camping out in the living room came as an unwanted surprise. It took some snooping to discover Sarah Bell adopted Lauren. My gaze returns to my sleeping angel. We had more in common than I thought. Bribing Xander into hacking into court records stacked my debt higher with him, but the information concealed in those documents proved worth it.

I lean closer, inhaling softly, her floral scent easing the bands of tension in my chest. My doll locked those memories away, a box no therapist proved capable of unlocking. A four-year-old Lauren wandered deserted streets, a ratty bear clutched in her small hands. People didn't get involved in business that didn't concern them, but someone called the police and child protective services scooped her up.

Sarah Bell worked the emergency room the night police found

Lauren, malnourished and abandoned. She filed to adopt my angel less than a week later and visited the foster home every day until a judge approved her request.

I want to kiss her, to burrow into her skin and erase the scars gouged into her mind. My tongue long to trace lips that never uttered the secrets of whatever hell she endured as a child before Sarah.

I force myself to pull back, taking several deep breaths. Soon, I'll take my angel with me. I tire of lurking in shadows, watching from afar. The need to touch, smell, and taste her became unbearable. Coming here jeopardizes not just me, but Zaine and Xander as well.

Reckless. Stupid. I agree with those self reclamations, but my muscles loosen in Lauren's oblivious presence.

Soon, I mouth to her, rising from the bed, stepping softly toward the door. I award myself one last fleeting glance. My fingers clench on the doorknob beneath my hand. I can't wait to hear her breathy moans in my ear again.

Calling on the last dregs of self-control I possess, I pull the door open and step out into the living room.

LAUREN

I shoot awake in bed, heart thumping a rapid beat in my chest. Sweat coats my skin. Throwing my thick comforters off of me, I plant my feet on the soft carpet beneath them. Wind brushes across my skin, making me whirl around at the open window I definitely remember locking. I rise cautiously from my bed, the carpet shushing my movements.

A quick look outside reveals lit streetlights, wet concrete from the recent rainstorm, and no shadowy figures staring up at me. I don't know why, but I sigh, disappointment flavoring the sound. I close the window, locking it, then double checking the lock. My body turns, placing the wall at my back, sliding to my butt on the floor.

Across from me, the off-white wall boasts my nursing degrees in gold frames, highlighting my accomplishments. My chest tightens, constricting. Fingers curl into the soft carpet beneath me. Every night since the EMTs found me, I've woken in a cold sweat, expecting to find Xavier standing above me. So far, that hasn't happened.

What worries me is I'm not sure if I'm disappointed or relieved by that. My body still sings from his cock bringing me to new heights, redefining pleasure for me. He's insane and a killer. It's just a physical response to stimuli, I remind my body for the hundredth time since returning to my version of normalcy. My ears listen for the sound of my mother's quiet breathing in the living room, interspersed with soft snorts. The woman denies she snores in her sleep. It's almost endearing when she embodies perfection in my mind.

An orphan couldn't wish for a better mother than Sarah Bell. I stride toward my bedroom door, thinking some water might cool my mind and body down. My feet pause, eyes mistakenly seeing moving shadows in my living room. I can't move, fearful that I'm not seeing things. I swore I saw a shape move around my living room, disappearing behind the black curtains gracing my window.

Deciding Sarah didn't raise a wimp, I race to the window, pulling the curtains aside. Chills and goosebumps abrade my skin. This window leading to the fire escape shouldn't be open, but it is, and I thought I saw a glimmer of a pale blonde head disappearing out of view. My nipples harden into greedy beads, but I force myself to lock the window, heart in my throat.

Sarah jumps up, screaming behind me. I whirl to face my mother, who has her hand clutching the neckline of her nightgown. My brows raise questioningly. This woman assured me she'd protect me, staking out in my living room, but screams at the sight of the back of her adopted daughter's body.

My hands find my hips, as I turn, glaring at my mother. She glances at me shamefaced, hands coming up to smooth her hair.

"Sorry, honey, you scared me." I hum noncommittally, deciding to return to bed. My eyes land on the front door and I decide to check it after tonight's events. I'm still uncertain if my mind is playing tricks on me.

I keep a gasp to myself when I find the front door unlocked. My fingers tighten on the knob, eyes closing. I don't know how to feel. Everyone claims Xavier kidnapped and raped me, that my denial is proof of a compromised mental state. I didn't need them to spell out Stockholm Syndrome to me. My own nursing knowledge informs me they're probably right, that there isn't a set time for when it kicks in.

I'm having a hard time convincing my body that Xavier isn't for me, a danger and a criminal. He haunts my dreams and taunts my waking thoughts. Locking the door, I head back to my bedroom, deciding not to tell my mother about the potential break-in.

When I collapse back into bed, my mind is already reliving the night he claimed me as his, his cock sliding in me slowly. I shudder, falling into dreams of him.

Stalker

LAUREN

TWENTY

"Are you sure you're okay, honey?" My adopted mother asks over brunch. I gaze unseeing out the wall-to-wall windows to our left. My food sits uneaten, picked at, on my plate. I barely tasted the mimosa my mother ordered for us. My fingers absently tug at the edge of my turtleneck. It's sleeveless, but the high collar hides the fingerprints fading from my neck.

I give her a weak nod as an answer, not bothering to voice the thoughts in my head. They make little sense to me, either. A prickle of awareness races across my spine. I stiffen in my seat, glancing frantically around the restaurant, eyes searching for pale blonde hair. My spine slouches into the seat with disappointment. No, I reprimand myself. It's good that I don't see Xavier around and haven't in a week.

I still can't shake the feeling of being watched, however. Sarah continues talking, paying little attention to my inattentive behavior. After returning home, she's been stuck to my side like glue. I love my mother, but I'm craving more independence, despite the chill following me everywhere I go. At first, it was a comfort having her crashing on the sofa, running into my room when I cry out in my sleep, sobs wracking my body. What I was crying out for, I couldn't say, but everyone assumed its trauma from the rape.

I shift uncomfortably in my chair, the high-backed cushion turning to steel bars in my mind. The police and EMTs found me naked, bruised, and cum leaking out of me. Of course, everyone assumed Xavier raped me. My protests that it was more complicated than that fell on deaf ears. Rape and kidnapping were additional charges lobbed against Xavier, who no one has been able to find. My instincts tell me he's nearby, watching me, plotting my punishment for letting them add more charges against him.

My walls clench on air at the thought of Xavier punishing me, instead of the fearful response I should have. Something's wrong with me. I must be sick in the head for having enjoyed Xavier pounding me into the ground, cutting off my oxygen. But I came hard enough to see stars, something no guy before him accomplished. Like a drug, my body craved it again, the absolute control he possessed over my body, his supernatural knowledge of how to get me off.

"Can we get the check?" I ask my mother, interrupting her tirade. I need to get home, maybe even scratch an itch. She nods, but concern shines in her eyes. I ignore it. She wouldn't understand. Hell, I barely understand it. Something shifted the night after Xavier's cousin arrived. Sighing, I conclude it must have been Stockholm Syndrome. Medically, it was the only diagnosis that made sense.

When the server arrives, I insist on paying, reminding my mother she needs to head into work. I'm on medical leave for three months, as if three months could restore my trust in the justice system. My body may crave Xavier like a drug, but it didn't erase the fact the prison failed me. I could never step foot in that place again without a panic attack threatening to overwhelm me. I just haven't put in my resignation yet, accepting the paid leave until I find another job.

∼

Tension oozes out of me when I'm back in my apartment, kicking off my shoes at the door. I could barely drink in the restaurant, but I make a beeline for the wine in my refrigerator, carpet brushing the soles of my feet. After undergoing several hours of questioning and examinations, I returned home relieved for having carpet, the lushness soothing my aching feet. They've healed up nicely since then, with little scabs I'm tempted to peel off.

Opening the refrigerator door, that feeling of being watched returns. I swing around, finding no one glaring at me on the other side of my one-bedroom apartment. Gray blackout curtains stare back, blocking the sunlight from invading my sanctum. A grey sectional lounges in the living room, nearly taking up the entire space. The granite counter behind me sits next to the stainless stove, no wall separating the kitchen from the living room, providing an open view of the space.

I remind myself that I'm home alone. No one is watching me. My gut says otherwise, but I've been ignoring it. I don't trust it after Xavier. He fooled me in the prison, and turned my body against me, craving him with increasing fervor. I think I'd drop my panties immediately if he walked through the front door. The wooden door remains stubbornly locked.

I walk myself to the sectional, searching for the remote so I could watch mindless television. Frowning, I notice the black device resting under the glass coffee table. That's odd. I remember placing it next to the television on the entertainment stand. Walking over, I drop to my hands and knees, reaching for the remote.

Something shifts in my peripheral vision, stiffening my spine, nearly hitting my head on the table. Someone is here with me, I know it. My heart races, fingers grazing the remote. I whimper, fearful to turn around, wishing for Xavier's protective presence. He might have been crazy, but I trusted he'd stand between me and any incoming threats that didn't come from me.

I slide from underneath the table, quickly rising to my feet and coming face to face with my worst nightmare. A masked man glares at me with familiar pale eyes. Before I can scream, both of his hands reach out, clamping a cloth around my mouth.

Damn it, I think, not again, before darkness swallows me.

Another Game

LAUREN

I awake sluggishly, blinking groggy eyes to focus on the sight in front of me. Pulling my hands forward has my head jerking upward, noting the metal handcuffs circling each wrist. My heart races with fear coursing through my body, until I realize I recognized the eyes of my captor. Closing my eyes, I force my breathing to slow.

I'm handcuffed to a table, each link attached to the four legs of the table beneath my back. Cool wood presses into me, jolting a weird adrenaline into my veins. Xavier stripped me, laid me bare on the table, handcuffed and spread eagle. My senses heighten, wetness pooling between my legs, desiring to be filled by him again.

I'm shaking my head, denying my arousal when I hear a door creak open, soft steps shuffling into the room. A glance down my body reveals a tall figure, dressed in all black. The ski mask still adorns his face. He closes the wooden door behind him slowly, letting me see him lock it. Silence stifles the room, neither of us speaking but watching the other, waiting for the next move.

My head moves with my eyes, tracking his slow approach. Black fingerless gloves conceal his hands. He trails those fingers up from my ankle to the inside of my thigh, eyes locked with mine the entire time. I should be afraid. I tell myself I don't want this or enjoy his sick games.

But I can't fight the moan that slips from me when he dances those fingers across my slick folds, finding my center easily. My hips jerk up eagerly. The cuffs clink with each movement of my body. My moaning fills the bare room, one fluorescent bulb shining down on my naked body. I'm quickly reaching the crest of my peak when he snatches his fingers away.

Pissed, I glare at him. I don't know how I know it, but I can tell his lips are curving behind that mask in a sadistic smile. He enjoys toying with me, and this is the ultimate game.

~

He brings up his damp fingers, shaking one of them in the universal no-no gesture. My chest rises and falls rapidly, a mixture of fear, expectation, and excitement swirling in my gut. Xavier walks away from me, stalking toward a second door. White tiles wink from the light that he flicks on in what I assume is a bathroom.

I hear him shuffling around in the bathroom before coming out with two objects in his hand, widening my eyes. I'm getting a sense of his game, suspecting it is his version of punishment. He still hasn't spoken and neither have I, unless my moans count. Soft steps stride toward me, scuffing the wooden floors beneath his boots with each step.

He stops, laying the chrome anal plug near my spread legs. My lips suck into my mouth as I eye the cylindrical toy remaining in his hand. The garish all pink looks horrible in the flimsy light in the room, but I recognize a wand massager from several videos I've watched. I don't own one myself, but trepidation flares within me.

Xavier uses his free hand to pull the ski mask off, revealing the golden bronze stubble coating his jaw, aristocratic nose and full lips.

Artic blue eyes pierce me, seeking beneath the marrow of my bones for my soul. Suddenly, I'm not sure I want to play this game. Malice twinkles in his eyes down at me. The hand holding the mask drops it, reaching for my breast, coaxing the brown nipple into a peak.

My teeth dig into my lip, trying to trap the moan. Genuine fear for my sanity and soul re-surges. His head drops, flicking his tongue out to tease my nipple. His groan at the taste of my skin relights the fire he fanned earlier. My eyes miss his hand bringing the wand between my legs, too busy rolling upward when I feel the first vibration. Pleasure crashes into me, cut short when he turns the wand off, tearing his mouth and wand away.

Smiling, he looks at me while licking my juices off the hand. I'm panting, needy for more.

"Do you want more?" he asks softly, appearing to read my mind. I give him a hesitant nod, uncertain of his motives. His hands bring the wand back against me, but doesn't turn it on yet.

He confesses his intentions, dread and lust warring for dominance in my heart. "I'm going to break you, Lauren, until all you desire is me. I'll hold the keys to your pleasure, become your addiction, like you are mine." He leans closer, the scent of me wafting off his breath. "I'm going to own you after this, and no one is going to be able to tear you from me."

Insanity and obsession carve lines into his face, etching the emotions into stone. I'm so screwed, is my last coherent thought as he switches the wand back on, bringing me to another powerful climax.

Claimed

LAUREN

TWENTY TWO

Time passes in an endless loop of Xavier wrenching orgasm after orgasm from me. Sometimes he even dares me to not come, knowing fully well the inevitability of him bringing me to a screaming climax. He played my body so well that I had no choice but to admit he owned it.

The chrome plug remains inside my ass. I lost count of how many times it nearly slipped out when Xavier used the wand or his tongue to make me come. He had to unshackle my legs to place them on his shoulders while his tongue relearned the shape of my pussy. Through my delirium, I noticed he enjoyed simply sticking his tongue inside me, letting my fluids coat his tongue like a favored flavor. He'd walk his fingers to my clit, making circles with those deft digits while staring up at me knowingly.

Sometimes I screamed I hated him, and other times I screamed I belonged to him. Exhaustion tugs at me now, insisting I find sleep. I whimper at the throbbing in my clit, the swollen organ being the recipient of excessive attention.

A shirtless Xavier walks out of the bathroom, his winged tattoos catching the light, a towel held in his hand. His full lips are a swollen shade of red. But he curls them in a salacious smile, prowling closer with the towel. I have zero energy left, limp limbs resting on the table.

Xavier laughs, reaching to wipe the mess between my legs. Only he possesses the ability to make me squirt. I almost cry when he wiggles the plug out of me slowly, my body used to the familiar sensation of clamping down on it.

"Loosen up, angel. I don't want to hurt that precious hole. I want to claim it someday," he says. Whimpering, I turn my head to the side, trying to relax, letting the plug slip out of me under his easy pulls. He lets out a victorious, "ah ha!", tossing the plug onto the floor. I feel his eyes on me, turning my head to gaze at him.

"You look worn out, doll. Do you want me to unchain you and carry you into the main house?" He speaks the words casually, but I detect vulnerability in his voice. He taunted me during all of his torment, my ears learning the smallest shift in his tone. A part of my mind thinks I'm not the only one claimed after our extended play time.

I nod my head weakly, the heavy weight rolling uselessly to the side after performing the task.

"Great," he says, pulling a key out of his pocket. I catch the movement from the corner of my eye. I hear the cuffs clink and click when he unlocks them. But I remain in my spread-eagle position, too weak to move.

"This won't do, angel. I'll be right back." I watch him stride back into the bathroom, returning with a plush bathrobe. A small whimper escapes my lips when he wraps me in the softest robe I've ever worn, gently pulling my arms through. Tears well in my eyes at his gentle aftercare.

If I wasn't so sore, I'd regret he hasn't put his cock in me since the night we separated. My brows furrow, eyes watching him pull me to his chest, lifting me into his arms. Happiness suffuses his face, beaming down at me. My head lolls against his chest, my eyes shutting out his happiness. My chest twists painfully, snarling at me.

I'm too confused, my mind and body a wreck with Xavier as the captain, carefully picking up the pieces. I admit to myself that I want to hate him, unable to summon the emotion when he's cradling me to his chest as if I'm precious to him. My eyes droop on the walk, not taking in our surroundings.

The sandman whispers in my ear, claiming me while I'm snuggled in Xavier's powerful arms, warm skin of his muscular chest, somehow trusting he wouldn't let harm come to me. I don't know when that developed, but I don't look at it, taking the sandman's hand, letting sleep claim me.

TWENTY THREE

LAUREN

Groaning at the aches and pains assailing my body, I roll over onto my back, blinking up at the etched ceiling above me. I frown, piecing together the fragments of my memory. My head turns to the right, the sound of feet striking the floor luring my attention. Xavier prowls closer. The vee of his hips draws my eye, disappearing into silky blue pajama pants. Unconsciously, I lick my lips.

A soft laugh startles my gaze to Xavier, heat flaring in the glacial depths.

"Are you ready again so soon?" He smirks, lips stretching wider. I blink at him, remembering the first time I saw that smile on his full lips. My brow furrows as I think my way through what I want to ask.

"Why did you take me?" I croak. I clear my throat of the sandman's influence.

"I already answered that, angel." The bed dips beneath his weight, rolling me toward him. I'm still weak limbed and don't fight gravity. Calloused hands land on my hips. A muscled abdomen contracts as Xavier finish shifting his weight onto the bed before releasing my hips and pulling me into his chest. I hear the deep inhale as he sniffs my hair. I probably smell like sweat and sex.

"Yes," I mumble against his warm skin. "But they imprisoned you six years ago. What changed? Why now, of all times?" I press. Some buried instinct claws at me for answers, needing to know the devil I'm entangled with.

He sighs into my hair, arms tightening around me.

"They denied me early release for good behavior. Again." Bitterness lace his words and I feel the tension lining his body. My eyes blink lazily. My mind processes his statement but doesn't reach an optimal conclusion.

Before I could open my mouth, he forges on. "I overheard one of the guards asking you out." His hands tighten their grip. "In my mind, I begged you to say no, but you didn't. I realized if I didn't get out of there soon, I'd lose you to someone else." His hands smooth up and down my back as if reassuring himself I'm real and in his arms.

"I didn't want to have kill another man so soon after being released for murder." My eyes drift to the curve of his lips.

"You could've tried harder to get early release," I tell him, trying to reach the humanity buried beneath his layers. My mind rushes through all the visits he made to my clinic leading up to his escape. Every scrape I helped heal. The frequent fights didn't tell the story of a man who wanted early release. "You stopped. Why?" My eyes search his, acting as a searchlight for the truth. I need this. I can feel a shift hanging in the wind, waiting with bated breath.

"Because she said I had no remorse, and she's not wrong." His expression smooths and I watch shutters clamp down in the windows of his heart. He's shutting me out, even as he holds me next to him. He's a walking contradiction and I can't help but wonder who hurt him.

"The first time they denied you was four years ago," I whisper into his skin, bringing my lips forward to kiss his chest. I want to reassure him, he can tell me.

"You stopped trying when you met me." Silence chokes the room as I admit the truth that he lacks the courage to speak. *I am the reason he stopped being on good behavior for early release.*

Nails dig into my skin before retreating. "Why do you ask questions to which you know the answer?" He barely restrains the snarl in his voice. His lips twist into a scowl, ice hardening in his gaze.

"Why don't you give me a straight answer? Or better yet, tell me why you did it!" I fire back, feeling the coals of anger sparking a flame. I could run, I remind myself. And yet I'm lying next to my captor, giving him the opportunity to open to me, to explain. Tears well and I dash them away angrily. He wrung screams and orgasms from me. I'm drawing the line at eking out more tears.

"Lauren—"

"Tell me!" I snap. He brings a hand to my throat, tightening infinitesimally.

"Will you stay?" I blink at him. My mind jumps from the tense conversation to the softly whispered question.

"Will you give me a reason to?" My eyes shift down. I don't know why I ask and can't risk witnessing whatever emotion will cross his face. His hand pulls me closer, his lips claiming mine, teeth nipping me softly.

"I'd give you the fucking world if I could, Lauren," he confesses against my lips.

"Just don't leave me." His breathing comes faster and his eyes drift open, searing me with his intensity. Wounded blue eyes bore into mine, wariness warring with vulnerability. "Give me time." His nostrils flare and his eyes close. Three sentences. I lean up to kiss his closed eyelids. Beggars can't be choosers and it's better than the attempted shut-out from a few moments before.

"Don't make me regret this, Xavier." I pull away, feeling the tension increase in his limbs. But I simply roll over and back my butt until it rests snugly against his cock. Exhaustion tugs at me, and I let the intensity of my emotions drain away.

There's always tomorrow and tonight, I admit to myself, was progress.

~

XAVIER

A split lip, three bruised ribs, and a glance down reveal busted knuckles. I take stock of all of this, ignoring the blood leaking from open cuts to leave a trail in my wake. My feet shuffle forward over the squares of linoleum, chains rattling with each movement.

Two burley guards maintain a grip on each of my arms, both to secure a flight risk and to keep me from falling flat on my face, adding a broken nose to the mix. My tongue swipes along my teeth, a metallic taste filling my mouth. I guess I've got bleeding gums to add to the list. I'm not looking forward to seeing Helga, as I call her in my head. The prison nurse stands easily eye to eye with the tallest inmate, who's nearly seven feet tall. A permanent scowl twist thin pink lips and her stiff nurse's outfit leaves a lot to the imagination, except for those full shoulders of hers, the wet dream of every quarterback in the leagues.

My ass is still smarting from the steroid shot she gave me last week. A needle doesn't need the full strength of your body weight to pierce flesh. It's been a shit week and a visit with Helga adds to the shit sandwich I'm gulping down, like my last meal. My eyes blink rapidly, weak limbs trying to keep my weight upright. I don't want to think about my broken family outside these brick walls and twelve feet tall chain-link fences. The last letter I wrote ripped open wounds I thought had healed cleanly. I was wrong.

The guards don't bother knocking on the nurse's door, shoving it open and practically throwing me through it. My feet skid across the floor, shackled hands shoot out to catch my weight on the raised examination table in the middle of the room. The nurse doesn't turn around at my abrupt arrival, for which I'm grateful, eyes traveling up from black leather shoes to the roundest ass in America, hugged by black scrub pants.

My cock jerks happily behind the zipper of my jumpsuit. My cock and I are both delighted it isn't Helga bent over the computer desk, gazing intently at the screen. Dark curly hair brushes a slender neck. Saliva pools in my mouth and I'm reminded I haven't seen a plump ass since before my incarceration.

She hasn't turned around, and it makes zero difference to me. Whoever the hell she is, I want her.

TWENTY FOUR

LAUREN

Warmth brackets my back, seeping into my skin, and calloused fingers pet the curls between my legs. I frown, my mind slowly coming online while my hips shift forward, pressing into the fingers lightly fondling me.

"Good morning, angel," a husky voice whispers in my ear, lips skimming across my skin. I shudder, leaning into the touch and seeking more contact with his fingers. Sleep clogs my throat so I don't bother croaking back a raspy good morning, humming into the soft pillow beneath my head.

Xavier laughs softly, the sound slithering over me, raising goosebumps. His laughs vary with his moods, and I can't pinpoint when I started taking enjoyment in guessing the meaning behind his laugh. He sounds sated, pleased with waking up next to me, curling his fingers against my slit.

I should feel appalled at his blatant disregard for my consent, but sometime during the night, I transformed into a needy, pleasure-seeking creature. My nipples tighten and my wetness coats the fingers circling me, easing me toward a gentle climax. I come softly, pleasure rumbling into me, sending me pushing against Xavier's bare chest, rocking my hips on the cock pressing into my back.

Xavier hisses, bringing his hand to still my movements.

"Let's head downstairs and meet everyone," he murmurs into my ear. Frowning, my eyes blink, taking in the opulent bedroom. A shocked gasp slips from my lips, noting the elaborate carvings on the walls. They're reminiscent of Victorian carvings, all raised edges and detailed etching. My jaw drops while taking in the beautifully molded walls. A large vanity rests near the door, sporting an actual marble countertop, an elegant high-backed chair, and the various perfume bottles spread out on the table look expensive from here. The room screams wealth.

My head shakes in bewilderment, wondering where we are and how Xavier came about such wealth. The questions tease my tongue. Xavier's hand slaps one butt cheek, eliciting a shocked gasp, core pulsing at the mixture of pleasure and pain, aftershocks still traveling through my body. Teeth nip my ear, breath fanning my neck.

"Behave, doll. Let's get ready and head downstairs. I want you to meet my brother," his voice catches on the word "brother" and I wonder if I should fear this unknown sibling of his. But the warm skin pressing into mine, lined with muscles and fingers decorated with callouses reassure me of Xavier's ability to protect. Sometime during our brief interlude, my body thawed toward him, trusting him with its wellbeing. My mind remained slow to catch up to my body.

～

XAVIER

This is happiness, I think, inhaling Lauren's natural floral scent. My mind wonders if it's the conditioner she uses or her own natural musk and pheromones luring me in to take another breath. I arrived at Zaine's door a mere three days ago, acting quickly to secure my doll. But tension still chokes the air when Zaine and I are in the same room.

I'm hoping Lauren and Zoe's presence would ease the tension, allowing us to shift toward an echo of how we used to be before I went to prison. A muscle ticks in Zaine's jaw whenever we're in the same room. I'm not sure if he's even aware of it. He hasn't informed our mother that I'm crashing in one of the guest rooms, yet. He was even more reluctant to allow me to use the guest house, eyes twitching whenever I asked for access and Zoe's cheeks turning a slight pink, eyes averting mine.

I wanted to know the reason behind his reluctance and Zoe's reaction, but suspected I wouldn't get a satisfying answer. My lips remained shut, jaw clenched, eyes demanding Zaine's capitulation. He capsized twenty-four hours ago, the reason unknown, but I suspected Zoe's imminent delivery played a role. Her belly appeared to swell overnight, like she'd swallowed a watermelon.

I would watch her with morbid fascination, waddling around the barren two-story house. Paintings decorated the walls, and the rooms boasted the same furniture, but it all lacked a personal touch, except for the nursery Zoe spent a considerable amount of time toiling in, painting the walls or setting up baby furniture, like bassinets.

My mind tempted me with images of Lauren swelling with our child, belly as large as Zoe's, a glow suffusing her cherubic face. My cock jerks against her, liking the image, whispering for me to fill her with my seed. I resist, just barely, pulling away and rolling until my feet land on the tiled floor beneath me. A scowl twists my lips at all the evidence of wealth, preferring something more humble or simplistic.

My chest tightens, the knowledge that I needed to clear the air with Zaine souring my mood. I think that this is why I don't pray to a deity. If such a being existed, I wouldn't have gone to jail to begin with, but also, my twin wouldn't detest my presence, our bond strained thin by his wife's presence and the years yawning between us.

I miss him, I'm loathe to admit. My back remains facing Lauren, mind swirling with countless thoughts. The thought of her meeting Zaine or becoming a member of my family never entered my mind when I snatched her on impulse. Now, I craved it with every fiber of my being.

I just hope I don't lose her before I can make that craving a reality.

Breakfast for Four

LAUREN

Metal forks clink against glass plates, the only sound breaking the stifling silence in the sterile kitchen. Chrome appliances and marble countertops catch the light from the chandelier in the ceiling, casting shadows on the occupants at the kitchen counter, sitting stiffly in high-backed chairs.

Eggs miss my mouth, falling to the porcelain China breakfast plate, and I stare down at them mutinously. My ears listen for the sound of conversation, but only the sounds of multiple mouths chewing answer me. I withhold a sigh, picking up the fallen piece of scrambled egg.

Xavier's body warms my left, elbows brushing mine, his quiet chewing a steady comfort. Déjà vu assailed me when I first came face to face with his twin, Zaine. His shy partner beamed at me from his side, hands caressing her swollen belly and assuaging some of my anxiety. Our skin tones matched, settling some internal tension I didn't know I possessed. Zaine and Xavier appear as Draco Malfoy twins out of a GQ magazine, making me feel small when Xavier isn't looking at me like I'm his entire world.

Tension hangs heavy in the air. Zoe doesn't say much, cleaning her plate with downcast brown eyes, curly hair pulled into a chic bun that I'm envious of. My eyes dart to Zaine's tattooed fingers, bringing on a flush, imagining Xavier's calloused fingers circling my clitoris, wetness pooling between my thighs.

We all continue to eat in silence until Zoe makes a noise, setting her fork down. Zaine abruptly pushes his chair back, appearing at her side in a blink, rubbing circles on her back with one large hand. I'm watching, wide eyed, Xavier's body freezing beside me, tension leeching from his solid form to mine. Zaine's blue eyes bounce around the room before stilling on his wife.

Zaine croaks, "I'll call the doctor," emotion clogging his throat. Xavier pushes his seat back, clearing his throat. Twin pale aquamarine eyes stare each other down.

Xavier offers, "Xander probably knows a doctor and my Lauren is a nurse. So, either one can get help and you can get Zoe settled upstairs." An uncertain expression flickers across his face before he adds, "Or you can call whoever you want. We can get out of your way." The softly spoken words curl around my heart, driving daggers into the organ and spurring me into action.

"My mother is a certified doula and I've worked a rotation on the maternity ward. We can help." My voice rises and falls in the room, insecurity leeching into my offer of help, making me cringe internally. Xavier's hand finds my back, smoothing large, comforting circles into the skin through the borrowed shirt that drapes my short frame, falling to my knees.

Zoe nods eagerly, both hands clasped around her swollen abdomen. Envy pricks me, but I shove it aside, slipping into a familiar professional role. I bark out instructions, expecting the twins to obey, rising to my feet and guiding Zoe to hers. She shoots me a grateful smile, obediently following me upstairs to where I assume is her bedroom, shared with Zaine.

Accomplices

LAUREN

My hands move with a will of their own, fluffing the pillows resting behind Zoe's back. The other woman sighs, hands massaging her bump. Words fail me so I look around the room, noting the bedside bassinet and changing table pushed up against the wall near the bathroom. An elaborately carved wooden door conceals what I assume is a closet. The walls boast the same carvings decorating the room I woke up in beside Xavier. The house wouldn't have been my first choice, but the architect did an amazing job.

Remembering my bedside manner, I ask Zoe, "Do you need some water? Where's your pain? Can you describe it to me?" My hands are already moving to palpate her abdomen, not waiting for permission. I pause an inch away, looking at Zoe wide-eyed. She laughs, a musical sound like trickling water. Her whole face lights up, positively glowing. My lips curl upwards in a contagious smile.

The uniqueness of the situation doesn't escape me. I'm torn between disappointment and surprise Zoe hasn't asked me about my relationship with Xavier. I remind myself there isn't a relationship to ask about, making a mental note to call my mother and reassure her, she doesn't need to call the cops on Xavier.

"This must be a lot for you to take in," Zoe muses, kind eyes roaming over me. I nod, heart clenching and wanting to pour everything out. She gives me a contemplative look before speaking again.

"Zaine kidnapped me too," she says, looking away from me. I catch her ears turn a slight pink, but shock tangles my tongue, trapping the words. I can't believe my ears.

"And you stayed!" I exclaim, brows rising to my hairline. She laughs again, round cheeks creasing her eyes.

"You're still here," she points out, waving a hand at me standing near her bed. I don't concede her point, struck mute by her bluntness. My eyes narrow on her suspiciously.

"You knew Xavier took me from my home without my consent." When the words leave my mouth, anger chases them, burning through me.

"You all knew he had me chained to a table and—" I break off, fighting a flush and a blooming arousal, thinking of the pleasurable torment Xavier put me through. Zoe reaches a hand out to placate me, but I step back, suddenly needing to be anywhere but near Xavier and his family.

This isn't my home and having breakfast with these people while sitting next to my kidnapper goes beyond Stockholm Syndrome. My feet carry me about the room, guilt pricking me at having upset Zoe when she's expecting and experiencing pain.

My hands slam on the bedroom door. Rusting sounds float to me and I half turn to Zoe, shooting her a glare. Her feet pause an inch above the floor.

"Don't you dare get out of that bed. You're pregnant. I'm the one having a mental crisis, but that's not a good reason for you to endanger yourself or your child. Get back in that bed, Zoe." My words come out harsher than intended to my ears, but Zoe obeys, shooting me apologetic eyes. Tears sting my eyes, and I blink rapidly to prevent their departure.

I walk back to Zoe, heart splintering and twisting into knots. I can't in good conscience abandon her in need, but I vow to let Xavier have it when we're alone again. Vindictiveness plagues my mind with all manner of ways to make him beg for my forgiveness while I continue assessing Zoe, barreling over her apologies. She's an accomplice, but she doesn't deserve my ire.

No, I'll save my fury for a certain criminal.

XAVIER

TWENTY SEVEN

Xander called me an idiot about ten times during our phone conversation, wind coming through the line as he rushed across town, cars honking in the background. He also threatened to leave me sitting in prison next time. I'd laugh, but his words sent foreboding tingles down my spine. I can't let anyone separate me from Lauren. My hands itch to kill anyone coming between me and my doll.

But Lauren's mother is a doula and if I plan to claim her daughter as mine, then she'd have to meet me, eventually. In my mind, its two birds killed with one stone. My future mother-in-law is coming to help Zoe, even though she doesn't know it, and she gets to meet me face-to-face so I can let her know for certain that Lauren is mine. I almost laughed at her shocked gasp when I told her I'd snap Lauren's neck if she brought the cops. I remember saying similar words to my doll, as if I could live a life without her in it.

Zaine wears a hole in the carpet, eyes darting frequently to the ceiling as if he could see through it to Zoe's condition.

"Lauren is an excellent nurse," I reassure him. Memories of her calm demeanor and professional bedside manner while tending to me flickers in my mind. Her lush lips would twitch with a smile when I taunted her, but she'd stay on task, documenting and cleansing my injuries before stitching me up. My cock jerks behind my sweatpants, wanting inside her again, craving her touch.

"If anything happens to Zoe or Zaria," Zaine grumbles, pale hair sticking up from several run-ins with his fingers. I step closer to my twin, taking in his lean build, tattooed fingers lacking scars, and his stance. My lips curl into an evil smirk, raking my gaze over Zaine. Logically, I'm aware he's concerned about Zoe, but his words trigger something feral within me, the need to protect Lauren from all threats.

Between one blink and the next, I pounce, kicking his legs out from under him. My fist connects with his face before he's rolling over, clocking my jaw. A snarl rips from me, hand coming around to punch him in the kidney. He yelps, locking a hand around my throat. Fuck this, I think, prepared to rip his damn dick off.

"What the fuck?" a voice screeches from the doorway, drawing our attention. My eyes widen, taking in my appalled mother in the doorway, plastic bags hanging limply from one hand. I grin at her, blood staining my teeth.

Meeting The Family

LAUREN

TWENTY EIGHT

A commotion from downstairs seeps through the door, drawing my gaze from between Zoe's legs. A sheet draped over her thighs, providing a tent, but enough light illuminated the fluids soaking through the bedding beneath her. I'm hoping Xavier curbed his murderous inclinations, because he's about to become an uncle in a few hours.

Zoe's water broke midway through my physical assessment, the noise downstairs breaking my concentration. I give her a questioning look, but she's wincing from an intermittent contraction. She admitted to having them for several hours, falsely assuming they were Braxton Hicks.

My hands smooth the sheet down, covering her intimate parts. Sighing, I wipe my hands down the shirt Xavier loaned me.

"I'll go see what they're up to. Were you planning on an at home birth or should we get you to the nearest hospital? And is there family we should call?" Zoe shakes her head, stray strands falling from her bun, kissing her cheeks.

"Zaine is the only family I've got," she whispers, bringing her hands back to her stomach. "And this little one." Her words send a pang through my heart, her loneliness calling to mine. I have a loving mother who didn't need a man to adopt, and she embodies perfection. Sarah Bell remained a tough act to follow behind, leaving me drowning at times in my own insecurities.

I soothe a hand over one sheet cloaked thigh, understanding some of the draw she must have felt toward Zaine, his complete adoration of her visible to anyone with eyes. Patting her thigh with one hand, I motion toward the door with the other.

"I'll go let Zaine know you're going into labor and you two can decide what you want to do." Brown eyes blink rapidly, a tremulous smile curving her lips. She nods at me.

After giving her one last look, assessing her comfort level, I march toward the door, curious about what the two kidnappers are up to.

~

Lost in thought, I nearly collide with an older woman walking down the hall, arms laden with folded towels. She peeks apologetic green eyes at me. I give her a shy wave, wondering if I should know who she is.

"I'm Tessa," she says by way of greeting, her head jerking toward the room I just came out of. "Does Zoe need anything? Zaine said she's not feeling well." Concern twists her weathered face, wrinkles pulling taut. I'm curious why Xavier never mentioned her.

"She's in labor," I confess. Tessa gasps, hands fumbling, nearly dropping her neat stack of towels. My hands reach out to steady her. In a split decision, Tessa drops the towels, scurrying into Zoe's room. Indecision grips me, but I decide the most important task is informing Zaine of his girlfriend's condition.

I stride down the curving staircase, admiring the artwork on the walls, following the sound of raised voices. My feet carry me to a sparsely decorated living room a few feet shy of the kitchen. My eyes widen, taking in Xavier's busted lip and Zaine's bleeding nose.

Another unfamiliar face turns at my approach, shocking me with her similarities to the twins.

I don't need anyone to tell me I'm staring into the eyes of Xavier's mother. We stare at each other in silence, my feet pausing in the doorway. Footsteps pounding my way turns my head toward Xavier's approach. My mouth opens with questions, but he closes the distance between us, claiming my lips with his.

His tongue strokes mine before retreating, pulling away with a less bloody grin gracing his lips, and a metallic taste coating my tongue. I want to kill him, especially when I hear the front door opening, my mother's voice calling my name from behind me.

She's Mine

XAVIER

TWENTY NINE

I can't help it. A cackle erupts from me upon spotting the enraged brunette striding through the front door, Xander tight on her heels. A white lab coat flaps behind her, acting like wings. She reminds me of a harpy, high-pitched voice screeching at me to get away from her daughter.

My back faces my mother and twin, catching my mother approaching in my peripheral vision. A cream pantsuit molds to her slim frame, catching the light as she steps around Lauren and me to intercept the screaming harpy. My grin widens at the chaos reminiscent of my time in prison.

The feeling of being grounded, of belonging right at home, circulates through my system, slow drops of blood still leaking from my split lip. My arm curls possessively around Lauren's generous hips, loving her curvy shape.

I watch with mounting excitement as my mother faces off with Lauren's. My doll pulls away from me, but I tighten my grip on her waist, fingers digging into her soft flesh through the material of my borrowed shirt draping her plump body.

She scowls at me, lips tempting me to lean forward and nip them with my teeth. She bites me back, tongue slipping across the cut in my lip. My hands slip to her rounded bottom, pulling our pelvises flush.

"Lauren! Get your disgusting hands off my child!" Lauren's mother screeches, spurring Lauren to tear her mouth from mine.

I narrow my eyes on the woman who's supposed to help Zaine's woman give birth, reminding myself I can't kill her. Yet. Lauren steps forward, but my mother's words stop her.

"My *son* could do better than your daughter. You should be relieved that someone like him would pay any attention to your offspring." I blink owlishly at my mother's words, mind slow to catch onto her meaning.

"What is that supposed to mean?" Lauren snaps at my mother's blonde head. I look to Zaine for help, sensing the situation's potential for blowing out of control.

He sneers at me, walking forward with his hands in his pockets.

"Mother, Lauren and her mother are here to help Zoe. And I didn't invite you." Zaine's contemptuous tone raises my eyebrows. My eyes flick from him to her, attempting to pierce the veil of their relationship with sheer will.

Tension lines my mother's shoulders, manicured nails curling into her hands to form fists. Lauren's mother steps around mine, stretching a hand out to my doll.

"Lauren and I are leaving. You people are sick and I'm calling the cops," she states, eyes pleading with my angel to grab her hand.

My patience snaps, feet hurrying me forward, wrapping a hand around Lauren's throat, bodily dragging her into me, cutting off her shocked intake of air.

"Lauren," I snarl at her mother, "isn't going any-damn-where. I warned you what would happen. Now, you will help us or you risk my doll's life." My fingers tighten, eyes locked with the woman wanting to take my prized treasure away.

Lauren brings her hands up, cupping them around mine, not even attempting to pry them off. I suspect she knows my bluff, my cock pressing snugly between her cheeks in the press of our bodies.

"Mom," she gasps around my fingers, "It's fine. Zoe's in labor—"

"What!" Zaine exclaims before darting out of the room, feet pounding up the stairs. I'd laugh, but Sarah Bell needs to understand Lauren belongs to me now. Smirking, I use my hand to pull Lauren's head up and back, making her lips easier to reach. I claim them hungrily, groaning into her mouth, bringing my other hand around to slide up her thigh, cupping her sweet pussy directly in front of her mother.

My doll moans into my mouth, tongue tangling with mine. Her hips jerk, seeking my fingers. I'm tempted to slide her panties aside and impale her on them right then and there, but barely resist. She has to face her mother after this, and I selfishly want the sight of her coming reserved just for me.

I pull my lips from Lauren but keep my hand beneath my shirt, her cunt pressing into my palm. My eyes clash with her mother.

"Lauren is mine," I inform her.My fingers slip beneath the seam of my doll's panties to trace her slick lips lazily, ready to prove just how much she belongs to me if I need to.

"Xavier!" Horror and embarrassment flush my mother's face. I can't summon the desire to care. Nothing and no one will come between me and my angel. In my mind, that includes both of our families. The sooner everyone understands that, the better.

"Ladies," Xander starts, striding forward and entering the fray. My chest eases when he comes into view between the warring women. Xander oozes calm, lifting both hands placatingly.

"A young woman upstairs is going into labor. Can we shelve this until mother and child are safe? Or will you have their deaths on your conscience?" Xander's blunt words choke the air, sucking some of the tension out of the women.

I release my hold on Lauren solely for Zaine and Zoe's benefit. My eyes track her mother's movements. Lauren fidgets with her shirt, smoothing the collar and hem. Conflicting emotions flicker on her mother's face, but she nods reluctantly, muttering, "Ok, let's get to work, honey."

Her hand gestures for Lauren to lead the way. My woman gives me one backward glance before following in Zaine's steps, her mother falling in step with her.

I watch them disappear from view, choosing to wait downstairs with Xander, who walks toward the kitchen. Thinking liquor sounds like a good idea to welcome the birth of my niece, I follow my cousin.

Baby Incoming

LAUREN

THIRTY

I avoid looking back at my mom, ears flushing a burning red. Arousal still courses through me, dampness coating the inside of my thighs from Xavier's teasing. I can't believe I let him do that, moaning like a nympho in front of the woman who raised me.

Sarah doesn't comment. She's a silent presence at my back, following me up the staircase. The stairs don't creak beneath our feet, showing off the architect's prowess again. When we reach the landing, I decide to address the kidnapper in the room.

"Mom—" I begin, but she holds up a hand, shaking her head, dark waves flowing across her shoulders. An implacable mask settles on her face. She says nothing, just gesturing with her hand for me to lead her to our patient. Despair sinks into the pit of my stomach. Blinking tears away, I nod, silently agreeing to hold off our discussion, but feeling disappointment rake across my nerves.

I think I've disappointed Sarah Bell enough for one day. Together, mother and daughter enter Zoe and Zaine's bedroom, donning their mental shields and stepping into the professional roles of caretakers.

Third Lasher

XANDER

Whiskey burns my throat and Zoe's pain filled screams echo through the house. A stiff chaise lounge cushions my back. I place a bottle to rest between my legs, wrinkling my khakis. At least I didn't spill a drop. Zaine remains upstairs with his woman and Xavier lounges on the matching chaise across the room from me, a bottle of vodka curled in his hand.

My black loafers shine from the ambient light of the chandeliers gracing the ceiling, elaborate molding providing a beautiful back-drop. I like the house, but I have to say I prefer my townhome across town. My mind wanders to Zaine, lips curving upward. He's not my favorite cousin, but I'm happy for him and Zoe.

Bile threatens to burn my throat, thinking of his suicide attempt seven years ago. I close my eyes against the memory, Xavier's sorrowful screams piercing my ears all over again when I broke the news to him. A dozen guards rushed him, wrestling him to the ground, screams ripping from his throat. One of the guards left to fetch the nurse he was obsessed with, with the goal of giving him a sedative.

I'd never felt more like a failure than I did at that moment. Countless sleepless nights culminated in being able to aid his escape.

But none of it made up for nearly failing to save Zaine. He was dead for two minutes before Zoe, the woman he kidnapped nearly a year ago, successfully resuscitated him. She's probably cursing his name now, opting to remain home for the delivery instead of having someone rush her to the hospital.

My eyes open, taking in the bruising blooming on Xavier's face. One arm supports his head, the other holding the bottle. He's staring up at the same ceiling I was moments ago. I think his presence may have influenced Zaine and Zoe's decision to have their child at home.

The women remain upstairs as well. Shock stiffened my limbs when Elizabeth Lasher agreed to stay, her and Tessa racing through the house fetching supplies. I made a couple of trips to the store so all hands could remain with Zoe.

Now, we wait for Zaria's arrival.

Hello, Zaria

LAUREN

THIRTY TWO

My heart stops in my chest, horror painting everyone's face when Zaria lands in my hands after a final push from Zoe. Deafening silence chokes the room. I act fast, snatching up a towel, hand held out to my mother for the suction. Once I suction any excess fluids in the little girl's nose, checking her mouth, I rotate her in my arms until she's lying flat against the palm of my hand. I pat her back, giving taps on each lobe of her lungs. Zaria gives a weak cry, testing her lungs before a shrill cry fills the room, a relieved breath easing out of everyone present.

I gently hand over the squalling child to her expecting parents, tears welling in everyone's eyes. My hands come up to my wet cheeks, wiping away tears. I jump when a hand smooths down my back. My eyes lock with my mom and I'm pulled into a hug, hearing Tessa and Mrs. Lasher congratulate the couple. A knock sounds at the door, a chorus of "come in" erupting at once.

My face stretches wide with a stupid grin when Xander and Xavier enter the room cautiously. My mom walks to Zoe, making sure all of her intimate areas remain covered, ever the considerate doula.

Xavier walks over to me, eyes never wandering to his newborn niece. Like a gravitational pull, I'm drawn into his arms, cheek resting against his chest. Something loosens in my chest. His hands massage the tension in my neck, lips brushing my ear.

"You want to get out of here?" he whispers. My head nods shyly, aware of eyes watching us. Xavier spares his brother a glance, shooting him and Zoe a wink before leading me out of the door, my mother's gaze boring into our backs.

For once, I don't care about disappointing Sarah Bell, seizing the opportunity to get Xavier alone. He has some explaining to do.

Escaping Xavier

XAVIER

THIRTY THREE

My hands find every excuse to touch Lauren. My thumb strokes the back of her hand from our entwined hands and my other hand itches to pull her against me again to claim her mouth. We make our way back to the guest bedroom given to me in silence. Lauren watches her feet, dark brows furrowed in deep thought. There are suspicious fluids staining the front of the shirt I loaned her and some of her hair escaped the plait she braided it into earlier.

To me, she's decadent, a treat I want to taste on my tongue, blood be damned. All too soon, we arrive at the door. I watch indecision play across Lauren's face. My instincts tell she's made up her mind about something, but I can't be sure what. I narrow my eyes into slits, wondering if she's thinking of running from me with her mother.

"You can't escape, doll," I tell her, tamping down the urge to throw her to the floor and remind her of what only I can give her. The Lauren I watched during our week apart, while I planned, was lonely. Few friends, no boyfriend, and only her perfectionist mother hovering around her. My angel was in a cage with no bars.

Her only escape is me and I will make sure she never escapes me.

When she glances up at me, her eyes lock with mine, a small smile curving her full lips. I step closer, but she steps back. A dance, I think. I like this game. Cat and mouse is my favorite game.

On Your Knees

LAUREN

THIRTY FOUR

I step back from Xavier until the wall meets my back. His body eases closer until his face hovers inches from mine. Excitement sparks in his eyes. His arms come up to cage me in, hands landing on either side of my head.

Just a week ago, being in this position with him would make my heart race for a different reason. Instead, I feel arousal dampening my panties, excitement zinging through my veins.

The moment has an air of inevitability, as if every moment before it led to this. I bring a palm up to rest against Xavier's chest, maintaining a distance between our bodies. My chin comes up, taking on a defiant tilt.

My lips stay curled as I slide my hand up to his shoulder, then applying downward pressure. His brows rise comically, pupils expanding.

"You want me on my knees, doll?" he asks, shock lacing his tone.

Keeping pressure on his shoulder, I nod, guiding him to his knees in front of me. Xavier grins sadistically, dropping to his knees, and then some. He drops to all fours. My heart drops into my stomach when I feel his lips brush across the tops of my feet.

What. The. Fuck. I can't breathe, lungs seizing on recycled oxygen.

He rises until he's sitting on his heels, still smirking up at me. How can someone kneeling still look smug? I wonder.

"Did you like me on my knees?" he asks, an odd glint in his eyes. I'm speechless, unable to speak or move, but he powers on.

"As I've proven, I'd get on all fours for you, doll. I'd crawl for you." His voice drops several octaves, his hands coming forward to glide up my ankles. He rises with his hands, words tumbling out of his mouth.

"I'd beg for you. Hell, I'd even kill for you," he whispers against my lips once he's at his full height, my shirt gripped in his hands, exposing my lower half.

I'm panting, breath kissing his lips, wondering how he turned the table, switching the game. I didn't even hear the trap closing around me until his tongue plunders my mouth. He uses my shirt as a leash, yanking me into him.

When I move to bring my hands into his hair, he steps back. I'm fearing the smirk tilting his lips. He clucks his tongue at me in mock disappointment.

"No, pet. I think you wanted to see me beg, to see me on my knees. Don't tell me you've given up already?" I shake my head, still struck mute, caught in his web.

"Well, doll, let's go into the bedroom," He gestures to the door at my back, "and make a beggar of me." A shocked laugh tumbles out of me, and I launch myself at him. He catches me easily, guiding my legs around his waist before yanking on the door and marching us into our room.

My tongue tangles with Xavier's, blocking everything out around us except the feel of his muscled body pressing into mine, cock teasing me with every step he takes, shifting with his movements. I hear the door close behind us, but don't pull my mouth from his. He kidnapped me, stalked me, but I never feel more alive than when I'm at his mercy, receiving whatever pleasure he deigns to give me.

I pull my mouth from his, lips swollen and pupils dilated with lust. Before the haze takes me, I want to bring Xavier to his knees. It's time for him to play my game. He's called the shots long enough.

My legs unwrap from his waist. His hands loosen, letting me slide down his body. My braid whips behind me when I whirl around, stalking toward the bed.

"Doll—"

"No talking," I call over my shoulder, kneeling down and feeling under the bed for the bag I saw him stash after laying me down the night before.

A dark chuckle sends shivers down my skin, more wetness dampening my panties. My lips curl mischievously. If I were being honest with myself, Xavier drew me in from the first moment we met. But I fought the pull with everything in my body, until he chained me to a ceiling, dismantling my defenses.

Now, I get to claim him as he claimed me.

~

When my hand lands on the strap of the duffle bag, I pull it toward me. Various toys bulge and overflow in the bag. I recognize the chrome butt plug and the pink wand. My eyes note the silver cuffs he used on me. Another piece of metal glints and I reach for it, a magnetic draw influencing my hand.

Xavier's soft steps pad closer, electricity sparking along my skin from his nearness. I turn my eyes on him, appreciating his lean physique, thick cock straining his pants, blue eyes capable of piercing my soul, blonde hair shaved on the sides, and lips capable of putting me in my place and bringing me close to Heaven's gates.

I remind myself he owes me, that tonight is about me. Blood and other fluids still stain the shirt he loaned me. I helped deliver his niece, despite not owing him a single thing. His reckoning looms and I will be its deliverance.

~

I pull my prize out of the duffle bag, shielding it behind my back and motion with my other hand for Xavier to climb onto the bed. I see the battle waging in his eyes, his desire for me and control warring with one another. The prize in my hand taps against my back as I await the verdict. For me, this moment is long overdue.

Clenched jaw and hands curled into fists, Xavier stalks toward the king-sized bed. The satin sheets shift and glide beneath his weight. Once he's comfortable, he looks at me expectantly. I give him a coy smile.

"Now, stretch your hands near the bedpost and do the same for the foot of the bed," I chirp cheerfully. Xavier scowls at me, a storm brewing in his eyes. But he silently obeys. I tuck my prize into the waistband of my thong, kneeling for the cuffs. It's high time to have Xavier at my mercy.

~

Metal clicks with a sound of finality, widening my smile, securing the cuffs around Xavier's limbs. Arousal and a feeling of authority tighten my nipples, my core throbbing to be filled by the blonde stretched out on the borrowed bed.

Xavier's hungry gaze follows me as I walk to the foot of the bed, pulling his shirt over my head. A choked groan fills the air, bolstering my confidence. I'm not a size six or below, but Xavier's impassioned gaze bores into me as if I'm the sexiest woman alive. I ignore the rolls lining my sides and the jiggle of my thighs.

His devotion makes me feel like a goddess, like Aphrodite herself. Cloaked in a lacy red bra and matching thong, I stand near the four-poster bed, gazing at the male specimen stretched out for me.

My hands pull my prize from my waistband, setting it near Xavier's feet. Predatory eyes lock on the blade, one brow cocked, but he doesn't comment. Smiling and feeling emboldened, I hook my thumbs into my waistband, dragging my thong down thick thighs. In Xavier's presence, self-consciousness has no place to sit, prowling the back of my mind. My unsteady fingers unhook my bra, freeing my full breasts.

My eyes track the jerk of Xavier's cock behind the cloth of his sweatpants. I can practically feel his desire wafting off him in waves. I feel desired, seen, and I want his cock stroking alongside my walls, bringing me to a screaming orgasm. But not before he makes amends to me. He owes me.

I pick up the knife and let my feet carry me forward, breasts and hips swaying with my movements. Xavier watches it all hungrily, gulping when I'm close enough to run my fingers along his cheek if I so desire. Instead, I press the blade of the knife against his throat, watching his Adam's apple bob with a hard swallow.

Conflicting emotions battle each other in both of our locked gazes. Lust urges me to climb onto the bed and straddle Xavier's hips. I do, but I don't rock against the cock beneath me. I lean forward, letting the knife nick his skin, watching blood well. Xavier eyes me like a starving man, desperation gnawing in his eyes.

"I already said I'd kill for you, doll. If you want me to die for you too, then go ahead, slit my throat. You got me where you want me, don't you?" His hips jerk beneath me, bucking my weight forward, making more blood seep from the deepening cut.

"Do it, angel. Slay your kidnapper and rapist." Tears well in my eyes at his words, my hands shaking around the blade. I want him, crave him like nothing else. But I despise what he did to get me. A sick, twisted part of me wants him to feel as helpless as I did hanging from that ceiling.

I could end him, but would that satisfy me? I wonder. No, it won't give me the same high as riding his cock, with him chained, only able to take what I choose to give. The knife clatters to the floor when I toss it aside. My heart races, and a smile curves my lips higher.

"What now, doll?" he whispers, never taking his eyes off of me.

"You will beg," I tell him before sliding down to remove his pants. My teeth nibble my lips as I glance from his spread legs to the cuffs securing his ankles. A smile teases my lips as I stride to retrieve the discarded knife.

"Angel?" Xavier questions. I bend over deliberately slowly, listening to air whistling between his teeth on a sharp inhale. I sashay back to him, smirking, fingers curled over the handle of the knife.

"What's your plan, doll?" He asks, swallowing deeply when I press the tip of the knife into the waistband of his pants. I think it is poetic justice that he's the one in the dark, anxiously pondering my next move. Gripping the knife between both hands, I jerk downward, watching the cloth separate until I come to the hem of one pant leg. I move to the other side of the bed, repeating the motion. Standing back, I admire the artistry that is Xavier's naked body.

My mouth waters at the thick cock revealed. I've felt it once, spasming around its thick length when he fucked me into the forest floor near the cabin he stashed me at. I'm hungry and impatient to feel it inside me again, but not before Xavier breaks.

I rock my hips along the hard line, my choked moan and his grunts filling the air. Wetness coats my thighs and opening, but I keep grinding on the cock I crave fiercely inside me.

I come, my walls clenching on air. Xavier's blue eyes darken, hips thrusting encouragingly. I shake my head at him, stray strands of hair sticking to my now damp skin.

King in Check

XAVIER

My cock aches, stained with Lauren's juices, straining against her lips to slip inside her wet tunnel.

"You want me to beg, doll?" I taunt her, eager to see how far my doll will go. Cheeks flushed, skin damp with sweat, she looks glorious. She'd look better riding me with her breasts bouncing with each shift of her hips.

She nods her head, still rubbing herself along my cock, keeping both of us soaked in her arousal. The musk of sex hangs heavy in the air. I inhale deeply. I want it from the source, my nose brushing her dark curls.

"Please, fuck me, angel," I whisper, a hint of desperation in my voice. I'll tear the entire damn place apart if she doesn't impale herself on my cock. Her soft hands tense on my chest, scrunching the material of my shirt. Her hips pick up speed and I know my girl is ready to come again, approaching that edge. I want her spasming around me, buried inside her.

"Angel," I coax, watching her pupils expand with every slick glide of my cock through her lips. She's torturing us both and I won't have it.

"What do you want me to say, Lauren? Hmm? You've got an agenda. Spill it." My hips shift upward on the next glide, trying to ease my tip inside of her. She gasps, moaning when it edges her opening. Instead of sitting back on it, she stills, looking down at me with those expressive brown eyes I could drown in.

"I'm sorry," I tell her. "I'm sorry I can't live without you, and don't want to. I'm sorry I forced you into this fucked up relationship, but I'm never letting you go. I'm sorry your life lacked something that you could only find with me. Baby, please, fuck me." My ass clenches from holding my hips up, keeping that tip inside of Lauren, praying my angel will put us out of our torment.

So slowly it'd test the patience of a saint, Lauren lowers herself onto my cock. My eyes close as she envelops me, walls twitching with each inch she takes. A muscle ticks in my jaw from clenching my teeth. I'm so close. Every muscle in my body tightens, not wanting to come before Lauren does.

I need her pleasure to force mine from me. I won't settle for anything else. Lauren mewls when she sits firmly on my cock, lips brushing my pelvis. She's taken all of me. Eyes closed and face scrunched up, she tempts me to give her one hard thrust to force her over the edge. But, my girl has claimed me. I know that's what this was and I won't take it from her.

She rises, gasping, slamming back down eagerly and repeating that motion again and again. At this point, my eye twitches from holding back. I can't help her along with my arms tied to the bedpost. A guttural groan scrapes my raw throat with the next hard slap of her hips, her ass bouncing against my balls. I feel like I'm holding back a dam with a sheet of paper.

Lauren's walls spasm around me. Taking the hint, I clench my ass again, shifting my hips up at the same time she comes back down. She screams, tightening around me, liquid gushing down my cock. I shout, cresting at the first tight press of her walls, cock twitching inside of her. Whimpers and moans spill from her as she grinds against me, too lost in her pleasure to ride me properly.

Still twitching, she slumps against my chest, panting into my shirt. Fuck. I never want to live without this angel, I think, letting my eyes close.

King in check. Well played, doll.

XAVIER

I blink bleary eyes open, smiling down at the angel resting on top of my chest. Planting a kiss to the top of her head, I gently roll her to the right. She grunts, frowning, and rolls onto her other side. I can't keep a smile off my face. If her mother stuck around for any extended amount of time after Zaria's birth, then she definitely heard her daughter getting railed, screaming at the top of her lungs.

Even now, my cock hardens again, wanting inside of my doll. Another creak outside of the bedroom door has me tensing. That's what woke me, pulling me from a pleasant dream of the life I'll make with Lauren. It won't be an entirely safe one, but it will be ours.

I slide out of the bed, smiling wryly down at the discarded cuffs Lauren removed after she claimed me. I quickly seized control and made sure she screamed my name throughout the night until her voice grew hoarse as vengeance for the dirty trick she played on me. But I suppose it was necessary. My Lauren never felt as if she needed anyone and we'd never be able to move forward if she hadn't felt like she reclaimed some sense of control.

My lips twitch with a smirk, knowing my doll secretly enjoys ceding control to me. My hands reach down for my discarded sweatpants. Still reeking of sex since I haven't showered, too busy remaining inside Lauren for as long as possible. I stride toward the door, not bothering with a shirt.

Before I leave to investigate the footsteps, I give one parting glance at my angel. Braid unraveling and haloing her head, plump cheeks rest on the pillow, lips slightly agape, letting out small huffs of air. I'm smiling, walking out of the door. At the moment, the only thing not right in my world is Zaine. Oh, and my status as a fugitive from the law.

I find Zaine striding up and down the hall, with a small, dark, curly haired bundle in his arms. He looks up at me, tensing. I watch him hug his daughter closer, protectively. I'm tempted to tell him to go fuck himself, like I'd hurt an infant. He relaxes his defensive position without a word from me, jerking his head toward the stairs.

My hand waves for him to go first. Fucker. He's had a shit attitude since Xander dropped me on his doorstep. Zaine frowns at me, but stalks toward the stairs, both hands supporting the babe sleeping in his arms. The house lay silent around us.

When our feet hit the landing in the foyer, I hear soft snoring coming from the sitting room near the kitchen. Ignoring Zaine, I march forward, wondering who's crashing downstairs. Elizabeth Lasher would never sleep on a sofa.

I push the door open, letting it swing gently on its hinges, and my eyes widen slightly. On one chaise lounge rests Lauren's mother, a crumpled white coat serving as a blanket. Xander snores on the other sofa, a couple of empty bottles littering the floor. I blink rapidly, cycling through foreign emotions. Xander, I expected to find still here.

Sarah Bell surprised me. Maybe that's what happens when you have a mother that cares about you, I ponder, stepping back to close the door. She had to have heard Lauren's screams of pleasure, but remained behind anyway, knowing her daughter enjoyed being in my bed, the man that kidnapped her.

Zaine watches me, gauging my reaction. I walk toward the kitchen, blindly letting my feet lead me forward. Stopping near the counter, trembling hands clutch it with a bloodless grip, fingers paling.

"She's her mother," Zaine whispers behind me.

"I know," I say just as softly, mindful of the child in his arms.

His steps barely disturb the silence as he walks around me until we're staring into twin pairs of blue eyes. My heart clenches painfully, the distance yawning between us. My other half. We shared a womb. I took hits for him. I served jail time for our mother, who didn't protect us.

My head droops, something inside me clanging loudly, breaking apart. Zaine comes closer, gripping one shoulder and holding the babe with his other arm. I can't bring myself to even ask to hold her, fearful I'd taint her innocence, just like I corrupted Lauren.

"Thank you," he whispers near my ear, coming closer with his bundle. I look up questioningly.

"For protecting me. I was angry at you for leaving me when I needed you. I didn't understand why you did it."

"Did Xander—" He shakes his head. His lips mouth "mom". The fucking floor drops from under me. My mother — I can't complete the thought.

"It used to be the two of us," I say, voice cracking.

"Now, there's five, not counting our mom, Tessa, Xander, and Lauren's mom." His words seep into my skin, burrowing through flesh. I test the word family in my mind.

My throat aches and I try talking around it. "We're a family," I croak, saying the words aloud.

Zaine smirks at me, squeezing my shoulder again. Family. I like the sound of it, just not the fear attached to losing them. My eyes close briefly, wondering how the hell a sick fuck like me got so lucky.

Keeping Xavier

The End.

Xavier and Lauren's story continues in Keeping Xavier, a short novella in the Sins of the Lasher Family series.

Here's your sneak peek at Keeping Xavier.

KEEPING XAVIER

My body rolls over, a frown twisting my lips when my hands land on cool sheets, satin kissing my palms. My eyes blink open in confusion. An ache between my thighs craves the shape of Xavier's cock while the rest of my body demands rest. But the criminal in question isn't lying next to me.

I bolt upright, sheets clenched against my breasts. A small, insecure voice taunts he took what he wanted and fled at the first opportunity. I push the voice away, sliding off the bed to my feet. Instinctively, I know Xavier's obsession burrows deeper than skin.

His lips whisper "mine" when trailing across my skin. Calloused hands grunts "mine", claiming me with each touch. Glacial eyes staring into mine while I gasp and moan, his cock slipping in and out of me, scream at me "you are mine". So, no, I don't think he abandoned me at the first opportunity, but I am battling the foreign feeling of missing another's presence. Before him, I preferred my solitude.

Now, it mocks my loneliness. Bare feet sliding against marble flooring echo in the hollow bedroom. Weak legs tremble with each step toward the bathroom, until the bedroom door slams open, causing me to freeze like a deer in headlights.

My eyes seek Xavier's angular face, tracing the full lips that buried between my thighs on more than one occasion last night. If capable of blushing, my skin would mimic a tomato.

"Xavier—"

"Where were you going, doll? Leaving me so soon?" An edge slithers into his voice as his eyes narrow on me and the satin sheet cupped to my chest, trailing behind me in a train.

Acknowledgments

Writing a book takes a village. I'm relieved to have found mine.

I'd like to extend special thanks to my editor, M.P. Starkweather. I'm sorry for springing a sequel on you but glad to have you along for the ride.

I'd like to thank Clare for roughing it out with an indecisive newbie author and getting my teams setup. Many thanks to my team as well who are invaluable to me. Your support is everything.

Elise, you are a superstar and will knock someone's socks off as a PA. I don't know what I'd do without your continued support.

I want to thank Poppy and everyone in our FB chat that extend their support and try to answer all of my questions.

I'll also like to thank you, dear reader, for taking a chance on an unknown author. Words cannot express my gratitude. I hope you enjoyed Xavier and Lauren as much as I enjoyed writing them. Stay tuned for Sins of the Lasher Family that includes Breaking Elizabeth and Training Xander.

Best wishes,
Mae

About the Author

Mae K. Knight is an emerging author of dark romances.

She lives in Louisiana and can be found studying for her nursing degree or powerlifting when she's not dreaming up stories. She believes she has a morbid sense of humor and tries to incorporate this into her writing

Her books will take you on a wild ride you never asked to embark on. Buckle up. If you like your twisted romances with a dash of taboo, you've arrived at the right place. Enter Knight's den of inequity. Only the depraved enter and the brave leave...